GW01086964

DEATH IN THE WASTELAND

George Bellairs (1902–1982). He was, by day, a Manchester bank manager with close connections to the University of Manchester. He is often referred to as the English Simenon, as his detective stories combine wicked crimes and classic police procedurals, set in quaint villages.

He was born in Lancashire and married Gladys Mabel Roberts in 1930. He was a devoted Francophile and travelled there frequently, writing for English newspapers and magazines and weaving French towns into his fiction.

Bellairs' first mystery, *Littlejohn on Leave* (1941) introduced his series detective, Detective Inspector Thomas Littlejohn. Full of scandal and intrigue, the series peeks inside small towns in the mid twentieth century and Littlejohn is injected with humour, intelligence and compassion.

He died on the Isle of Man in April 1982 just before his eightieth birthday.

ALSO BY GEORGE BELLAIRS

DEATH IN THE WASTELAND

An Inspector Littlejohn Mystery

GEORGE BELLAIRS

ipso books

This edition published in 2016 by Ipso Books

First published in 1963 in Great Britain by John Gifford Ltd.

Ipso Books is a division of Peters Fraser + Dunlop Ltd

Drury House, 34-43 Russell Street, London WC2B 5HA

Contents

CHAPTER ONE
A BODY VANISHES

The Maid wakened Littlejohn and told him he was wanted on the telephone. No peace for the wicked! He removed the newspaper which covered his face, eased himself out of the long lounge chair in which he had been extended, took a quick almost furtive swig from the glass of *Pernod* at his side, and followed the girl, down the long cool corridor like a cloister, to the instrument.

'Allô!'

An English voice answered.

'Is that Superintendent Littlejohn?'

Littlejohn and his wife were staying with his friend Dorange, of the Sûreté at Nice. Dorange, a bachelor, lived with his parents in their villa at Vence in the hills behind Antibes. His father was a wholesale grower of roses and carnations and their home stood in the midst of his gardens, bathed in the fragrance of flowers. Behind, the ground rose steadily to the barren forbidding peaks of the Basses-Alpes; ahead, it slowly descended to the Baie des Anges and the fabulous blue Mediterranean.

It was August and the air vibrated with the heat. Grasshoppers and cicadas were chirping in the fields and cars and motor-bikes kept up an incessant hum along the distant roads.

Littlejohn was on his own. His host was on duty in Nice; his father was in his rose-fields; and Mrs. Littlejohn and Dorange's mother had gone on a shopping expedition to Antibes. Littlejohn had propped himself in a chair in the shade of the loggia, cursorily scanned a three-days-old English newspaper, and then spread it over his face and fallen asleep.

'Is that Superintendent Littlejohn?'

'Yes.'

'My name's Waldo Keelagher...'

No wonder the French maid hadn't been able to pronounce the name! She'd called him Monsieur Kay, and then given it up.

'My name's Waldo Keelagher. You won't know me, but I happen to be a cousin of Inspector Cromwell...'

What next! Somebody on holiday who'd found himself at a loose end or else short of ready money. However, Littlejohn had heard of him. Cromwell had spoken of his cousin Waldo a time or two. He was a London stockbroker, who now and then gave Cromwell hot tips which didn't come off. Impossible to forget a name like Waldo.

'He's mentioned you from time to time. You're a stockbroker, aren't you?'

The voice grew full of eager relief.

'That's right. Thank God you've heard of me, and I don't need to start proving that I'm genuine. I'm in a mess with the police in Cannes. I'm there now. My car's been stolen. But that's not the worst. My Great-Uncle George's dead body was in it.'

Littlejohn mopped his forehead with his free hand. Either he or Waldo must be suffering from the heat.

Trundling his Great-Uncle George's dead body around the Côte d'Azur in a car! It just wasn't possible.

'Say that again ...'

'I know you won't believe me. It's fantastic, but ...'

There was someone else on the line, too, to add to the confusion. It sounded, judging from the arithmetical conversation, like a maître d'hôtel of a large establishment arranging his rake-off with the local grocer.

'Please hang-up. This line is engaged. Police.'

Littlejohn smiled as he said it. He could imagine the receiver of the unknown intruder being very softly replaced. There was a click and they were free of him.

'You were saying ...?'

'I'm sorry to bother you, sir. But, you see, I'm on holiday here with my wife and we don't know anybody. I'm in a fix. We were in a caravan. I ought to tell you that my Great-Uncle George insisted on coming with us, and died suddenly last night. We were miles from anywhere, and well ... I thought we'd better bring the body to the nearest town and report it to the police. It seemed the best thing to do at the time, but now I have my doubts. I brought him to Cannes, parked the car near the police station, and my wife and I came in and told them about it. They wanted to see the body. When I went out to the car, it had been pinched and the body with it. I swear that's the truth. The police here think I'm either mad, or playing a practical joke on them, or else perpetrating some hideous crime or fraud. They won't believe the car was stolen ...'

No wonder! Littlejohn wondered if he were having a nightmare and would wake up when it grew too horrible to bear.

A pause.

'Excuse me. The policeman here's saying something ...'

Littlejohn could overhear it. The quick-spoken French of the policeman was almost loud enough to be heard down in Vence. Then, Keelagher asking him in halting French to speak more slowly.

'He says I'd better ask you to come here and discuss the matter. He says he's sorry to trouble you. He's a friend of Commissaire Dorange and has met you before, but it's a rather awkward matter to settle over the 'phone.'

Awkward! If he hadn't been Cromwell's cousin ...

'All right. I'll come. It will take me about an hour. How did you know I was here?'

'I saw in the paper that you were in Vence staying with Commissaire Dorange. That'll be Cromwell's boss, I said to my wife ...'

Littlejohn might have known! The papers had got it and inserted it in the *Comings and Goings* column between a notice of the arrival of an oil magnate in his yacht and that of a film-star who'd run away with a conjurer's wife.

Superintendent Littlejohn and wife, of Scotland Yard, arrived yesterday, to stay at Les Charmettes, home of Commissaire Dorange at Vence ...

The trouble was, it was too hot altogether for undertaking a wild-goose chase after Great-Uncle George's body. It was only out of affection for Cromwell, who, for some reason, always seemed proud of cousin Waldo and his Stock Exchange, that Littlejohn bestirred himself and took out the little Floride which was at his disposal and snaked his way down to Cannes. He was almost killed twice on the way. Once by a car with a large G.B. on the back, driven by an Englishman who seemed to have gone berserk and reverted to driving on the left. The other was by a Frenchman, driving at sixty and trying to make love at the same time.

When he reached Cannes, he wished he'd stayed at home. The streets were packed with holidaymakers manipulating every possible kind of vehicle, one main street was blocked by a religious procession and, in the other, a milk lorry had apparently collapsed beneath its load of bottles and scattered milk and broken glass all over the shop.

The police were therefore fully extended and the disappearance of Uncle George, deceased, had become a side issue. He found Waldo Keelagher sitting with his wife, despondently neglected and waiting in a small room for attention. Even the good looks of Mrs. Keelagher, a straight-haired, blue-eyed blonde, with a skin the colour of honey and next to nothing on, had failed to stimulate the local officials, the bulk of whom seemed to be noisily concerned with the milkman who'd blocked the Rue d'Antibes.

Waldo himself looked as excited as he probably did in Throgmorton Street after a substantial change in the Bank Rate or the collapse of Wall Street. He was tall, fair and slim, and his thin yellow hair was plastered across his head as carefully as if he'd just returned from the City. His features were distorted by a huge pair of sun-glasses, which he removed when Littlejohn entered to reveal his panic-stricken eyes and eyebrows so pale that he didn't seem to have any at all. He was dressed in a sleeveless buff shirt with shorts to match and his body had the boiled look which arises from too much sun.

The arrival of Littlejohn was like water in the desert to Waldo. He flew at the Superintendent, too full of emotion to speak, and wrung him heartily by the hand.

'So good of you,' he said in a broken voice.

Waldo's wife, who was very beautiful, and seemed intelligent with it, too, was taking it all very calmly. After all, it wasn't *her* Great-Uncle George who'd died and been stolen.

Also, she was of a different temperament from Waldo, nervously exhausted by the ups and downs of stocks and shares. She provided the morale of the partnership and Waldo the money. Besides, Great-Uncle George, now, they hoped, with God, had been reputed to be worth a quarter of a million, to say nothing of the goodwill in the stockbroking firm of which he had, until lately, been senior partner and in which Waldo carried on the family name. The thought of Uncle George's estate gave her a comfortable, warm feeling inside.

'So good of you to come, Superintendent. We do appreciate it. I'm in a real mess. I don't know whether or not it might end-up with my being accused of murder...'

'Don't be silly, darling. Of course it wasn't murder. Uncle George ate far too many mushrooms last night and his heart gave out. Now that the Superintendent is here to help us, everything's going to be all right. Isn't it, Superintendent?'

It just depended on what you meant by all right. Little wonder the Cannes police had been incredulous...Here they were now, in the shape of a *brigadier*, who, as soon as he saw Littlejohn tactfully vanished and was replaced by an Inspector. Littlejohn had met the Inspector before. His name was Joliclerc.

Joliclerc, who had once worked with Littlejohn in Cannes on a case of a murdered English antique dealer, was delighted to see him. So much so, that Waldo Keelagher's dilemma seemed forgotten and the meeting took on the form of a social function. Joliclerc shook hands with Littlejohn three times before they finally got down to work.

'Yes; the matter of Monsieur Valdo...Valdo...'

Inspector Joliclerc looked at the card on his desk.

'Valdo Kaylayjay...'

It would do! Anything to get down to business and get away.

The Inspector confessed that he didn't understand English. And Monsieur Valdo's French was a bit difficult. He thought that perhaps the Superintendent Littlejohn wouldn't mind coming to interpret and help Monsieur Valdo.

So, the three-cornered interview began. Waldo to Littlejohn in English. Littlejohn to Joliclerc in French. And then the return journey to Waldo.

As Littlejohn expected, it took some time to convince the French police that Waldo wasn't drunk or mad. This formality finally overcome, Joliclerc sent for a male stenographer to take down a statement. He politely allowed Littlejohn to do the questioning, only intervening now and then to elucidate a point.

It turned out that Waldo Keelagher was a great do-it-yourself votary and over the past two years had been building a luxury caravan in his spare time. He had finished it in the Spring, tried it out at Easter to Swanage and back, and he and his wife had voted it good for a trip to the Riviera in August.

Late in July, Waldo had committed the folly of boasting about his handiwork to his Great-Uncle George, the wealthy head of the firm in which he had made Waldo a junior partner. Anticipating the ultimate arrival of a family, Waldo had prudently planned accommodation for four in his vehicle.

'The very thing!' Uncle George said when he heard of it. 'I'll come with you.'

Waldo paused in his narrative at the horror of it, and Littlejohn paused for breath in his marathon translation to Joliclerc.

'You see, Uncle George, who is about 65 ... or *was* ... besides being a stockbroker has for a long time very vigorously carried-on a hobby and since he went into semi-retirement, it's become a sort of mania. He's a naturalist and writes books about it. He's just started another. It's about what's called the praying mantis...'

Praying mantis... It stumped Littlejohn as interpreter. However, Waldo had a note of the French for it in his diary among a lot of other phrases supplied by Uncle George.

La mante religieuse! Joliclerc and his stenographer threw up their hands in chorus, shrugged, and looked more stupefied than ever at the mad tale. Waldo continued as though it were an everyday occurrence. He seemed to be talking to himself.

'... It seems that, although Uncle George had closely studied these insects in captivity... he had a sort of praying mantis zoo in a gauze cage... to study them properly he wanted to see them in their natural habitat, as he called it. He said the fully developed adult mantis made her appearance on the Riviera in August, like the rest of us. He said with a caravan, we could camp right among them, so to speak. He was bad on his feet and said the hotels were too far away...'

'He was too greedy to pay his hotel bills, in spite of his money. He was a miser,' interrupted Mrs. Waldo, whose name, by the way, was Averil.

'What does madame say?'

Littlejohn translated and Joliclerc smiled for the first time during the tale. And, seeming to notice Averil, too, for the first time, he twisted his little moustache and straightened his tie. The more acute stenographer had already done this half-dozen times.

'He insisted on coming. It was difficult, in fact impossible, to say No to him. You see, I work for his firm and, well, he's a very wealthy man.'

He paused and coughed.

'Go on, Waldo. You may as well tell them. You have expectations...'

Waldo turned pale and then flushed and, as though dazzled by his forthcoming good fortune, put on his dark glasses again.

Littlejohn thought it high time to control the narrative. After all, they couldn't be at it all day. It was nearly lunchtime, too.

'He came with you?'

'Yes. We tried our best to persuade him out of the idea, but he was always a stubborn old man. Do you know, the praying mantis eats its mate in a most revolting manner...'

No wonder all the hot tips Waldo gave Cromwell always ended in a washout! He simply couldn't concentrate on the business in hand.

'When did you set-out?'

'Last Saturday. We stayed on Sunday outside Beauvais. On Monday...'

'When did you arrive in Provence?'

'Tuesday. We camped just outside Aix-en-Provence. Yesterday, we arrived very early in the Estérel, where uncle proposed to spend some time studying his damned insects. It's wooded there, and stony, and we'd no trouble finding a spot for the night. Averil and I went down to the coast for a bathe at Théoule and left uncle hunting for mantises. We got back around six in the evening.'

'You found him safe and sound.'

'Yes. He said he'd had a splendid afternoon. The place, according to him, was teeming with mantis. He'd also gathered a lot of mushrooms. They looked lethal to me, but both Averil and uncle said they were all right. He ate a lot after Averil cooked them in milk and I think that's what upset him.'

'What time did you retire?'

'About nine o'clock. It was dark then and there was no pleasure sitting out of doors with a light. The place was infested by every kind of winged insect, especially mosquitoes.'

'Your uncle slept in the caravan?'

'Yes. There are two bunk-rooms, a kitchen, and a bathroom and toilet.'

At the translation of the sanitary arrangements, the two Frenchmen threw up their hands again. Joliclerc looked baffled and interjected a private question at Littlejohn in in an undertone.

'Do they have water-tanks and do they carry the water to them to operate the bath and the W.C. in the wagon?'

'Yes.'

Joliclerc shrugged his shoulders sadly. He was obviously dealing with madmen and told the shorthand-writer in a whisper to take account of it.

'You passed a good night?'

'Averil and I are good sleepers. We'd had a heavy day. We slept till eight. Then we got up and found uncle had passed away.'

His tone suggested that if Waldo had been wearing a hat, he'd have bared his head. It seemed to rile his wife.

'He was *dead*,' she added.

'Was he a normally healthy man?'

'Generally speaking, yes. He never ailed anything for as long as I can remember. But lately, he'd been under the doctor with a weak heart. He pooh-poohed the idea, of course. He was like that. He fancied himself as a quack-doctor, as a matter of fact.'

Littlejohn was beginning to build-up a picture of Great-Uncle George. Quite a character!

'He died in bed?'

'No. He was lying on his face outside the caravan, as though he'd been taken ill and gone out for fresh air.'

'Fully dressed, or in his pyjamas?'

'He didn't wear pyjamas. He said they made him feel suffocated. He had a nightshirt.'

'Was he wearing it?'

'No. He was fully dressed. We thought he'd had a heart attack. He must have been dead for some time. He'd gone cool.'

Gone cool! Joliclerc leapt to his feet.

'Why didn't you leave the body as it was and go to the nearest telephone and notify the police?'

Littlejohn translated, but Averil replied.

'Waldo lost his nerve and went all to pieces. I don't blame him. You'd feel the same. Miles from anywhere in that appalling country with nobody about. I believe it was once the haunt of brigands and cut-throats.'

'But that was no excuse for packing-up the body and bringing it to the police in that way. If death wasn't natural, you've destroyed all the evidence.'

Averil suddenly seemed to understand Joliclerc's angry, authoritative French.

'You can tell him he needn't get in a tizzy about it. I offered to go for help, but Waldo wasn't fit to leave or to drive either. We couldn't leave the body out there. It didn't seem decent. We seem to have done the wrong thing and got ourselves in a rare mess. I think we ought to have buried and left the body there, after all.'

Littlejohn translated a revised version of that. No use annoying the French police. Things were bad enough as it was. Averil was thoroughly annoyed with them all.

'I know it sounds silly to all of you now. Actually, it seems silly to me, too. But Waldo's had two nervous breakdowns since the war. He'd a bad time with the Gestapo as a prisoner in Germany. I wasn't going to have him down with a third breakdown. He's more precious to me than all your Uncle Georges. What did Uncle George want foisting himself on us, any way? He'd no business coming.'

'So, you made a parcel of him and put him in the caravan?'

'No. We locked the caravan, left it where it was, and brought him here by car. We knew he'd died a natural death. We're not medical experts, but who'd want to murder Uncle George at that time in the morning?'

Joliclerc put his head in his hands. It was getting beyond him.

'Go on ... *Continuez*...'

'Well, that's all. We brought the body in the car, as I've already told you. We parked outside and came in to report it. We knew there'd have to be some sort of post-mortem but it seemed simple to us then. We explained to the sergeant here, who brought in someone who understood English. Then we took them to where we'd parked the car. It was gone!'

Averil told it all in a very matter-of-fact way. Waldo kept trying to get a word in edgeways, but she wouldn't stop. She seemed to have made up her mind to get it over.

'And that was where you came in, Superintendent Littlejohn. Waldo had seen in a paper we bought at Aix that you were staying near Nice. We felt we needed some help.'

That was the end. Averil had been wound-up and now she'd run down. She burst into tears.

Waldo trembled, wrung his hands, hung over his wife and tried to comfort her. At first, Littlejohn thought he'd attack the French police. Eventually, he managed to quieten down the pair of them.

Joliclerc sat back and sighed deeply. He was a heavy man with a small moustache and sad, pouched brown eyes. A most polite and civil officer whose patience had been badly strained. He was moved by Averil's tears. He looked at his watch. One o'clock.

'We must send someone to the caravan and the spot must be examined. Also, give me details of the stolen car, which we will circulate. Do you happen to have a portrait of the dead man, too?'

Waldo produced various papers covering the car, as well as a photograph of it, coupled to the caravan, with Waldo proudly at the wheel and Averil with her head through the window. He also produced their joint passport and everything else he could think of. His driving-licence had been endorsed. Dangerous driving two years before! He seemed to think he owed them an explanation.

'It was the night before my wedding...'

Finally, Waldo probed in his wallet and produced a post-card photograph of Uncle George. Whether he carried it for good-luck or duty he didn't say.

Uncle George was dressed in academic cap, gown and hood. A small, shrivelled-looking man, with a hatchet face, Roman nose and shrewd piercing eyes. He had a tough, stubborn look about him and, on the occasion of the photograph, must have achieved some long-sought triumph, for he looked self-satisfied.

'That was taken nearly ten years ago. He got an M.A. degree for a thesis on Ants when he was nearly sixty.'

Come to think of it, Uncle George looked a bit of an ant himself! Industrious, persistent, a confounded nuisance...

Joliclerc swept the papers in a file and gave his orders to the secretary. He was quite unimpressed by the cap and gown.

'And now...'

He looked sternly at Waldo and his missus.

'If what you say is true, you are both in a delicate position. We ought to detain you until the matter has been cleared-up...'

Littlejohn told them in English what it all meant.

Waldo made a noise like a sob.

'In gaol?'

'Yes.'

His first thoughts were of Averil.

'I'm sorry, darling. It was all my fault. I ought to have been firm with him.'

Averil seemed to know how to handle him.

'Of course it's not your fault. It's your Uncle George's for insisting on coming and then dying on our hands. It serves him right.'

She turned to Littlejohn.

'I didn't mean that, but it makes me so mad. Could you help us, Superintendent? You've been wonderful, but there's one thing more. Could you sort of go bail for us? After all, you can trust us. Waldo's your Inspector Cromwell's cousin on his mother's side. Could you?'

Littlejohn couldn't refuse, could he? Cromwell's cousin! He spoke with Joliclerc, who seemed glad of a chance to do him a good turn.

'I'll have to speak with Commissaire Dorange to begin with.'

It took a bit of ironing out. They had to go higher up the ladder than Dorange for a final decision. Littlejohn ended-up in charge of Waldo and Averil. They were in his hands, *sous caution,* under bail, pending the clearing-up of the affair.

Littlejohn didn't mind being responsible for them. They were nice young people. Cromwell's relations. But, he had them on his hands until Great-Uncle George turned-up. And, perhaps after that, too.

He invited them to lunch as his first duty as godfather. It was like being guardian to a couple of kids in distress.

CHAPTER TWO
LITTLEJOHN BECOMES
A GODFATHER

They lunched in one of the restaurants in the old quarter of Cannes, on the edge of the port, facing the masts of luxury yachts and fishing-boats tied-up in the harbour. The heat of high noon was scorching and everybody seemed to be sheltering from it under anything which gave shade. Down at the water's edge among the boats a dog had gone mad, foaming at the mouth, rushing here and there snapping at passers-by, until a gendarme had finally drawn his revolver and mercifully shot it. A crowd had gathered round now that the danger was past and were discussing the event with great animation.

Waldo and his wife, the excitement of the morning ended, were now suffering from the reaction of events. They were more than ever like a couple of waifs under Littlejohn's protection. They didn't seem hungry, but he encouraged them to eat. He finally tempted them to a meal of freshwater crayfish with salad, livened by a bottle of sparkling white Burgundy and ending with iced petits fours.

After that, they were more disposed to talk freely. Littlejohn noticed, however, the caution of Averil where the wine was concerned. Waldo's glass was empty almost as soon as filled; her's remained untouched until, perhaps remembering she was Littlejohn's guest, she sipped her wine slowly and appreciatively, but never much at a time.

This beautiful girl had brains as well as good looks. Whether Waldo was naturally without initiative, or it had been sapped from him by the brutality of the Germans in the war, was a question. But Averil made up for the pair of them. Whenever Waldo seemed ready to talk too much or indiscretion hovered on the edge of his tongue, she took the conversation from him and replied with care and good sense. Looking into Waldo's naïve, tepid eyes Littlejohn easily understood his inability to resist Uncle George. He wondered, however, why Averil had tolerated him. It had obviously been diplomatic to do so.

They did not speak of the tragedy until the meal was finished. They contented themselves with watching the comings and goings in the sun-drenched port; the touts for craft plying for hire, the boats shuttling to and from the islands in the bay, the crews of luxury yachts busy aboard, but rarely putting out to sea, like captive insects patiently going through the same motions over and over again in an effort to be free.

The meal and the heat dispelled any desire of Littlejohn to pursue the case of vanished Uncle George. Like Waldo and Averil, he was now feeling a bit rattled at him for butting-in and threatening to spoil his holidays. In any case, how much longer was this going to last? The body might be anywhere now. There were plenty of lonely spots in the hills behind in which a corpse or even a car could be ditched for good. They might never see Great-Uncle George again.

In which case, how long was it going to be before Waldo and Averil were free to go? And when was Littlejohn going to be released from responsibility for the pair of them?

'Excuse me, but where do we go from here? Will we be allowed to go back to the caravan and sleep there till the police at Cannes have finished with us?'

Waldo looked really anxious, expecting they'd have to spend the nights locked-up in a cell.

'I really don't know. They might impound the caravan and bring it in for examination. Or, they might tow it along to the town and let you use it. In any case, I'm sure they won't allow you to go and sleep in it out there on the Estérel. It might be too much temptation for you to bolt.'

Waldo looked pained and shocked.

'As if we would.'

'I'm not suggesting you would, but you can quite see that the local police will have to take every precaution.'

'Of course. How long will they be before we can feel ourselves free to do as we like again?'

'I'm sure I can't say. They'll have to find your stolen car and they're on the spot where you camped now and will probably bring-in the caravan for examination…'

'Examination! You'd think we'd murdered him.'

'They've got to go through the routine formalities, Mr. Keelagher. You'll have to be patient about it. After all, it's *your* uncle. You'd be annoyed, I'm sure, if they simply treated the matter flippantly and told you to go and find the car and his body yourself.'

'I hadn't looked at it that way.'

Littlejohn was getting a bit bored with the situation. What was he going to do next? He couldn't even send them out for an afternoon's excursion. They'd no car! As for taking them a run-round himself, in the circumstances he felt he'd far rather lounge about in a waterfront café.

'Let's have a drink,' he suggested finally.

Waldo looked as if he'd had enough already. The heat and the wine at lunch seemed to be making him squint a bit. And whenever he wanted to make a point, he made slow-motion gestures like someone cleaning a blackboard. A sort of alcoholic emphasis.

'I think I'd like a glass of tea with lemon. Waldo likes that, as well...'

The way Averil said it sounded like an order.

Littlejohn ordered the tea for them and a *Pernod* for himself. Waldo seemed disposed to change his order and take a *Pernod,* too.

'I've heard of that stuff. A bit potent, eh?'

But Averil wouldn't let him have it.

Things in the neighbourhood were livening up again after the lunch break. A steady stream of cars was passing, drivers who showed any inclination to be casual suffering a string of moving abuse from the rest who seemed feverish to be getting along. Littlejohn lit his pipe and offered his guests a cigarette apiece.

'What made you think your uncle died a natural death?'

Waldo and Averil looked at him in surprise.

'Why not? You're not suggesting we murdered him, are you?'

He realised that he'd chosen the wrong topic of conversation, but the question was an interesting one. The answer might be useful later.

'No. But until the police discover something, it might be a good idea to turn matters over in your minds and try to remember any little detail you might have overlooked in your haste to get to Cannes with the body.'

'There's something in what you say...'

Waldo turned to his wife and gently made rubbing-out motions in the air again.

'*Why* did we think he'd met a natural death, darling? As far as I'm concerned, I never gave a thought to anything *but* natural death.'

Averil was quite cool and collected. She took up her spoon and mashed the lemon in her tea.

'There were no signs of violence about. He just looked as if he'd died naturally and quietly, that's all. I don't see there's any more to say about it.'

'Were there any traces of prowlers? Anything which might have wakened your uncle and made him get up to investigate?'

'No. As I said, he was fully dressed. We thought he'd wakened early and decided to take a walk, perhaps in search of more mushrooms for breakfast or even to pay an early visit to his insects. Do you think he died by violence, Superintendent? You keep harping on the matter.'

'Not really. I'm just interested and feel it will be as well to be ready if the police here ask you questions.'

'Well, we won't have any answers if they launch an inquiry of that kind, will we, Waldo?'

'No. Certainly not.'

Littlejohn was seeking the accurate picture which he always sought in his cases. The victim, his environment and a general idea which might bring him to life and living again in his familiar surroundings.

If he couldn't have Uncle George dead in the Estérel, he'd have him alive at home, then.

'Where did your uncle live in England?'

'Great Missenden.'

'Alone?'

'Great-Aunt Lucy lives with him. She's unmarried and two years younger than he. There are one or two servants, but Aunt Lucy keeps house.'

'Is that all the family?'

Waldo looked surprised.

'Of course not. Great-Uncle George had only one child, a son, William, who died in infancy. His wife left him, years ago.'

'What about the rest? Anyone of your generation still surviving?'

'You seem very interested in the family. Look here; this isn't a murder case, you know. I hope you aren't ...'

Averil intervened.

'Don't be silly, Waldo. Can't you see the Superintendent is just taking a kindly interest in you. After all, he's a sort of godfather to both of us, till the French police decide we're free to do as we like again. It's not much fun for him, being saddled with us. How long holiday have you still, Superintendent?'

'A week or so. I really came over on a police conference ... an international affair ... at Marseilles. I took a few extra days to call and see Inspector Dorange at Vence. He insisted on our staying as long as possible.'

'It's good of you. We'll try to be as little trouble as possible. Was that all you wished to know from Waldo?'

'If it bores him, yes. Otherwise, we may as well complete the family tree.'

Waldo seemed only too glad to continue.

'It's something to do, isn't it? I'm just wondering what we're going to do if the French police take much longer on this matter ...'

Littlejohn could have given them the answer. It wasn't likely the French police would leave them in Littlejohn's custody for long. The machinery for recovering the car would already have been set in motion and the police all over France would be on the lookout for it. If Uncle George's body were still in the car, cause of death would soon be decided. If it weren't from natural causes, Littlejohn would soon be free of his charges. They'd be lodged in gaol until the puzzle was solved.

'One thing at a time, Mr. Keelagher...'

'Call me Waldo, Superintendent. It sounds more homely in the circumstances. And my wife's name is Averil.'

'Thank you. Shall we go on where we left off?'

'The family? All right. Uncle George's only child, William, died early. There was my grandfather, Uncle George's brother. He had two sons, Rupert and Crispin. Uncle Rupert was killed in the first war, which left my father who was Crispin. He was a great fan of Ralph Waldo Emerson. That's where I got my name from. I have a brother, James Emerson Keelagher. He's in business in the City. Produce. He lives in a flat in the West End. He was married, but his wife left him and he divorced her. I think he's contemplating getting married again.'

'The lot?'

Waldo giggled.

'Not quite. My father had another uncle, Hubert, who went to Canada and had two sons. The eldest, Martin, is a Roman Catholic priest in Montreal. The other, Wilfred, had two sons, Peter and Conrad. Father Martin and Peter and Conrad are still alive. They're all in Canada. Peter is a farmer, I believe, and Conrad is in a bank. Now that Uncle George is dead, there's Aunt Lucy, my brother James, Father Martin, Peter, Conrad and me left. It's a funny thing, but there haven't been any girls in the family since Aunt Lucy.'

Littlejohn pictured in his mind one of those genealogical tables he used to swot in history books. A long line of Keelaghers, finally ending *Waldo, m. Averil...*

Waldo seemed to read his thoughts.

'We ought to write it all down. I will do, perhaps tomorrow. We'll probably have plenty of time together at the rate the French police are moving.'

'You mustn't complain about the French police, Waldo. You may be in for a surprise. They're very fast and efficient.'

'I hope so.'

'So you and your brother will probably be the principal beneficiaries under your great-uncle's will.'

'I shouldn't wonder. He's always been very good to me. He took me in his firm when I left school and has always kept an eye on me. Of course, he may have shared it out with Peter and Conrad and even included Father Martin with the rest of us. He's been to Canada several times to see them and Father Martin was in London and called on him last year. They seemed to give him a good impression.'

'Where do you and Averil live, Waldo?'

'Not far from Uncle George. Amersham. He bought us a house there for a wedding present.'

Averil intervened.

'That's an overstatement, Waldo. *He* found the deposit and *we* took out a mortgage. It's as well to be exact when dealing with the police.'

Waldo agreed that that was right. He always seemed to agree with Averil.

The conversation lapsed for awhile. They sat there watching the passers-by and the tempest of traffic.

'The police are taking a long time,' Waldo finally said with great impatience.

'Give them a chance. What about some more tea...?'

Tea came again and they started chatting over the cups. This time Waldo seemed to think it was Cromwell's turn for a pat on the back. He and Cromwell were cousins on the distaff side. His father had married Cromwell's aunt. They had kept in touch and Waldo seemed as proud of Cromwell's connections with Scotland Yard as Cromwell was of Waldo's stockbroking.

Someone was eating mushrooms on a nearby table. It seemed to give Averil a sudden turn.

'Mushrooms. I never want to see any again.'

'Were they the traditional ones that your Uncle George picked and ate last night?'

'Not exactly. But they were quite edible. I've had that kind before. Uncle knew them, too. Waldo was a bit dubious, but uncle and I managed to persuade him in the end. He enjoyed them. These were what are known as blewits and are regarded as a great delicacy in England. You can put out of your mind that Uncle George died from eating them. He ate more than us and it might have upset his stomach but they couldn't have done him any harm...'

The conversation was interrupted and things seemed to begin to move at last.

A small car, driven by a policeman, was slowly approaching them, running down the line of cafés and restaurants on the waterfront, as though the occupants were seeking someone. This manoeuvre apparently upset the consciences of one or two dubious-looking characters, some of them very respectably dressed, sitting in the open air, for they rose and vanished into the interiors. Finally the vehicle pulled-up opposite Littlejohn's table and the terror of all the malefactors of the Côte d'Azur stepped out.

He was a small dapper man, with a hatchet face burned mahogany by the sun. He had bright black eyes which shone with animation, and a perpetually pleasant smile. He wore an almost white suit, with a snakeskin belt and snakeskin shoes, and there was a red carnation in his buttonhole. A man on a neighbouring table who'd been too busy talking to his girl to notice what was going on, suddenly spotted the newcomer and covered his face with his newpaper. The little man tapped him on the shoulder in friendly fashion and pulled back the newspaper.

'Good day, Fred.'

The man had turned the colour of a lemon.

'Good day, Inspector Dorange. Nice weather we're having.'

'See it remains so, Fred.'

Littlejohn introduced his friend to Waldo and Averil.

'I've heard of you two, *mes enfants,* from the local police. I thought I'd better come over and see if I could help. I believe my friend Littlejohn has adopted you.'

Mrs. Littlejohn had been improving Dorange's English and they got along fine. Waldo's French was a bit confused, but Averil was rather a dark horse at the language. She seemed to understand all that was said, but either couldn't or wouldn't speak very much herself.

As Averil seemed to have forbidden Waldo to drink *Pernod,* they ordered beer all round and their glasses were empty before Dorange began to talk business.

'The Cannes police found the caravan in the place you indicated. It was apparently just as you had left it. They towed it to Cannes and it is now sealed and in the police garage awaiting examination.'

Waldo's mouth opened slowly.

'Sealed! But we'll want to sleep in it tonight. We've made no arrangements...'

'The Cannes police have made arrangements for your accommodation until they have gone into the affair. I had some difficulty persuading them not to hold you in the police-station itself.'

'Arrest us, you mean, and put us in the cells?'

'Exactly.'

It was as Littlejohn had expected, but thanks to Dorange's efforts it wasn't as bad as it might have been. But Waldo didn't seem to agree. He was white with fury. Averil put her hand on his arm.

'Don't go off the deep-end, darling...'

'I *will* go off! They've no right. I thought Superintendent Littlejohn was seeing to it that we were, at least, decently treated. As it is...'

Dorange tapped him sympathetically on the arm.

'Not so loud, young man. You don't want all the café to know your private affairs. The car has not yet been found. We will find it very soon. But matters are more serious than when you left the Estérel. The officers who went to the caravan also searched about to see if there were any clues or traces of how your uncle actually met his end...'

Averil nodded to Waldo.

'You see, darling, the police did believe us, in spite of what we thought...'

'Yes, they believed you, but, let us say, the manner of your telling the story of what happened rather bewildered Inspector Joliclerc. As I was saying, the police searched the neighbourhood of the camp you made. Someone, and we presume it was your deceased relative, had been sick in the grass not far from the caravan...'

'Didn't we say he'd eaten too many mushrooms and had probably got up feeling ill?'

Dorange nodded sadly.

'Yes. There were traces of mushrooms. The policemen brought samples of the vomit back with them and it has been provisionally analysed. There were substantial traces of mushrooms there. But that was not all. I am sorry to say that there were also traces of arsenic there, too.'

CHAPTER THREE
TIP NO RUBBISH

At first it seemed that Waldo was going to have a brainstorm. Matters were becoming too much for him. However, he quietened down after a while. The police had arranged for him and Averil to stay in a respectable private hotel near the station. The proprietor of the place was the brother of one of the police sergeants and would, therefore, exercise a mild and unobtrusive scrutiny of the pair of them.

'Sort of house arrest,' said Waldo bitterly, after he'd recovered his equilibrium.

The whole affair had become a great embarrassment to Littlejohn. The body of Uncle George might never be found, even if the car turned-up. If the car-thieves had unwrapped the ungainly parcel in the back seat and found a corpse, they'd quickly get rid of it. You could imagine their astonishment and fearful confusion when it came to light! The only hope was that they'd ditch it and the car together, and clear off as fast as their legs would carry them. Meanwhile, Littlejohn was saddled with the Keelaghers and perhaps the lot of them were becoming a bit of a bore to Dorange. Not that Dorange showed any annoyance. In fact, judging from his smiles and calm courtesy, matters like the vanishing of Uncle George might have been everyday occurrences in his life.

Furthermore, the case was too widespread for comfort. If Uncle George had died violently, but properly, at home, among his expectant relatives, friends and enemies, the local police might have narrowed things down. Instead, in a moving hotel on wheels, with everything to hand for cooking and poisoning his meals, he'd not only been sensationally ill and spewed up poison all over the camping site, but ended-up dead, in a stolen car probably abandoned Lord knew where.

And it had all happened in France, in the worst possible way and complicated by the stupidity of Waldo. The intricate international formalities were enough in themselves, without a murder case and a vanished corpse!

Now, to add to the confusion, Waldo's brother James was on his way, by air, to support his beleaguered family.

Waldo had insisted on their informing James, in spite of the fact that he and James didn't get on well together. To begin with, James had once been Waldo's rival for the hand of Averil and had taken her choice of Waldo in a most unsportsmanlike way. To console himself, he'd married a woman with money, who soon ran away from him.

'He's always left Uncle George to us in the past. Now, I'm not facing all these complications alone. James must take his share.'

'But he can't do any good here. He'll only get in the way.'

'I don't care, Superintendent. He can come over and do a bit of worrying about it, for a change. I didn't murder Uncle George. Neither did James, I suppose. So, he's got to take his part.'

Waldo was allowed to telephone James. They had a boiling row over the 'phone right away. James started blaming Waldo for not looking properly after Uncle George and, finally, for losing his body. It might have been a quarrel about a stray dog. James said that Waldo was proving himself as incompetent as usual and he'd better come over before he did something really stupid.

James made it plain that he couldn't stay for long. Just enough to straighten matters out, and then return home. James was in the pepper business and, at present, the market was tricky. Pepper was going up and down in alarming fashion. Just like Waldo to get himself in a mess like this ...

And, as a farewell shaft, James added that Waldo was a bit of a cad to lead Averil into such a silly escapade and if it hadn't been for her, he wouldn't have bothered at all about it and left Waldo to stew in his own silly juice.

'I like his damned cheek!' said Averil after Waldo had hung-up.

Waldo didn't need to pass-on a summary of James's conversation. His brother's booming voice travelled loudly all the way from Mincing Lane to Cannes and spread all over the room there, just as if James were shouting from an open window across the street. Dorange heard it all, too.

Littlejohn began to look forward to the arrival of James. Perhaps he'd take Waldo – and Averil – off his hands and prove to his sister-in-law what a bad choice she'd made.

Waldo, in spite of the telling-off telephoned by his elder brother, seemed more comfortable after it.

'James will be able to help. He has friends in the government.'

As though that would do any good! It was Waldo's way of excusing his brother for bullying him. Averil didn't seem impressed.

'Rubbish! What can he do if he comes? He must think that because he supplies pepper to the Admiralty, the

French are going to treat him like a VIP. He'll only annoy them and get Waldo steamed-up by his bullying...'

Evening was approaching and, as they couldn't remain with Waldo and Averil all night to advise and comfort them, Littlejohn and Dorange saw them to their hotel and left them to calm-off in their room there. James was crossing by the night 'plane, knew where his brother was staying, and would presumably erupt upon Waldo and Averil and the rest of Cannes in the early hours. After a day with his pepper, he was catching the 1.55 a.m. from Heathrow and arriving at Nice at 3.45.

'And see that there's a car there to meet me. I don't want to be stranded at that ungodly hour...'

Littlejohn said goodbye to Waldo, who was now worrying about his finances. He hadn't enough money to cover emergencies of this kind and Uncle George, who had promised to pay the bill for the whole trip, had vanished with the stock of ready cash and travellers' cheques in his pockets.

'You'd better stop worrying and get some sleep. Your brother will be here about half-past four and I don't suppose you'll get much more after he arrives...'

Nor would anybody else in the hotel, either, if James's actual voice equalled his telephoned booming!

Poor things! was Mrs. Littlejohn's comment when she heard of the tribulations of Waldo and Averil. Littlejohn made the same comment to himself when he met James the following morning.

When he arrived at the hotel with a queer-sounding name at which the police were lodging Waldo and his missus... Hotel Hellespont, that was it... Littlejohn felt he'd sooner loaf about the streets of the old town surrounding the railway station than go inside and become involved in the case of Uncle George again. It was early morning and the sun hadn't yet parched everything. In the station square, they'd been round with the watercart to lay the dust and there was still the smell of the water on the air, giving it a refreshing tang. From the little markets nearby he could hear the shouts of the stallholders and an easygoing crowd of shoppers were making their way through the glass doors of Monoprix and the shops around. A man who'd tried to park in a forbidden zone was quarrelling with a policeman and a couple of taxi-drivers were almost coming to fisticuffs about a fare.

'He's the biggest man in pepper in the City.'

That was what Waldo had said about James, as though it were something to be proud of.

James was very annoyed when Littlejohn arrived. Not about Littlejohn, of course. James said he appreciated what the English police chap was trying to do. It was the whole situation which angered James. First, the mix-up and vanishing of Uncle George. Then, Waldo's handling of it. Finally, the Hotel Hellespont was the last straw. He was furious with the Cannes police about the place and almost flew at the benign Inspector Joliclerc who'd taken Littlejohn in tow for the time being.

'It's a disgrace! A low place where you can't have a bath and the telephone's public and right in the hall where everybody can hear what you say...'

He was supposed to be speaking French, which, owing to James's fury was very fluent, but sounded more like Russian.

'What's he say?' asked Joliclerc.

The trouble was that James had decided to stay for the night and wanted a room with a bath. There weren't any. Then he'd asked for one with a private telephone, as he wished to keep in touch with London about pepper. There weren't any of those either.

'What's he come for?' asked Joliclerc.

'He's a London business man and wants to get matters settled quickly. He's more or less head of the family.'

Littlejohn looked absently round the room. It was a small place off the hall and hadn't any windows. It smelled of dust and was illuminated by a brass chandelier with yellow bulbs. The furniture was of the boudoir variety, probably bought at a sale, had once been pink upholstered, and now you couldn't quite put a name to the tint it had assumed. It had the atmosphere of a rendez-vous for spies or illicit lovers.

As for James, he disappointed Littlejohn, who, judging from his voice over the telephone yesterday, had assumed he would be a large man. Now, he turned out to be about five feet eight or nine, very broadly built, very aggressive, with shaggy thick eyebrows and thin black hair brushed back. He was very clean and well-groomed, in spite of his overnight travel, and he'd had a bath and a shave in the solitary bathroom on Waldo's floor, which overlooked the goods-yard where they'd been shunting most of the night. The bathroom was kept locked when not in use and you had to ask the proprietor for the key. James looked as if he shaved a lot and pulled the skin of his face about, for it hung in folds down his cheeks like that of a bloodhound. He was a bit bow-legged and walked like a cocky little cavalryman.

'Is everything all right?'

It was Battistini, the police sergeant's brother-in-law who owned the hotel, popping his head in with a civil question.

'No, it isn't?'

James's French was so bad that Battistini couldn't even understand *that*. He smiled, nodded, and went off as though he'd been complimented.

Moving among the rest of them, dressed casually in various kinds of holiday wear or, in the case of the police, their light summer clothes, James Keelagher looked as though he'd suddenly emerged from a band-box. A dark, pin-striped suit, white linen, and a dark spotted tie ... Probably just as he dressed when he went to the pepper exchange.

He'd already sent off two telegrams to the City and was now impatiently waiting for a 'phone call with the opening rates for produce and foreign exchange.

James sat on one of the boudoir chairs and looked at Littlejohn.

'I'm tired out, and I've got to get back for tomorrow night. There's a delegation in London from Ceylon and we're giving them a dinner. I've to propose a toast, so I must get away in time. How long do you think it will take to square matters up here?'

You half expected him to take out his cheque-book and say 'How much?'

'It's a silly business, isn't it, Superintendent?'

'Silly? I'm afraid your brother doesn't think so. He's at his wits' end. And as for your uncle ... I don't think he'd think it silly, either, if he were alive to judge.'

Littlejohn's steady look seemed to put James out of countenance. He pulled out a bunch of dog-eared papers from his pocket, shuffled them, and pretended he'd not heard the rebuke.

'Did you get on well with your uncle?'

James looked surprised. He hadn't intended matters turning out this way. He'd expected to find the police only too eager to hand over his brother to him, and to be able to take him and Averil home right away. What the French police did with Uncle George once they found him didn't seem to matter much.

'When did you last see him?'

'Last week. He called at the office and said he was going to the South of France with Waldo and Averil.'

'Why tell you?'

'He was that way. Anything Uncle George did was, to him, so very clever and important, that he thought he had to let all the family know.'

'Did he seem all right?'

'Never better. He started being unpleasant, as usual. Somehow, he always thought pepper was a good joke and made silly cracks about it. I told him whether it was a joke or not, it was my livelihood and I liked my work. He said he guessed someone had to look after the nation's pepper.'

James never smiled; just told his tale in a serious monotone.

The telephone bell rang in the hall.

'That'll be for me.'

James ran out. It wasn't; and James returned looking as though the bottom had fallen out of the market and his existence.

All the time, he moved and spoke with the utmost gravity. It was obvious that he was putting on a bit of an act for Averil's benefit. Showing her she'd picked the wrong man when she'd chosen Waldo. The broken reed instead of the go-getter.

'I've decided to go to Nice right away. I'll have a talk with the consul there. His brother's a friend of mine and he'll soon fix things for us and have you out of this.'

He gave Averil what he thought was a comforting look, but which seemed to cast her down more than ever. She was bewildered and had lost a lot of the initiative she'd shown the day before.

James seemed to think the whole problem could be settled easily by pulling wires in the right places. Like getting seats at the theatre when it's officially booked-up.

Littlejohn heartily approved of James's going to Nice.

'Yes; do that. The consul will, at least, be able to guide you as to procedure.'

The consul would also tell him how serious the matter was, the kind of affair that couldn't be settled in the club over a glass of whisky. At any rate, it would get James out of the way. Here, he was nothing but a confounded pest.

As Waldo was officially confined to the hotel, James went on his own. He ordered a taxi, after haggling about the price, and emerged with a brief-case under his arm as though he'd got the whole matter sewed-up and ready for off. He told Waldo to answer the 'phone if any call arrived whilst he was gone.

'Take down any messages word for word, then tell them you'll contact me and I'll ring them back. Say I'm on a deal in Nice. If it's vitally urgent, ring up the consulate and tell them to tell me and I'll ring you back...'

It took you all your time not to tell James to drop dead or else get going for Nice and keep going. There was a carnival of flowers there, to which Littlejohn had missed taking his wife, all because of Uncle George. He hoped that James would get mixed-up in the carnival, go completely off the rails, and get himself delayed for a day or two on a round of dissipation...

As soon as the elder brother was on his way, Joliclerc suggested that Littlejohn might like to see the impounded caravan.

The caravan! Littlejohn had forgotten all about it.

When Waldo heard it mentioned, he asked if he could go, too. He sounded like someone asking to be allowed to visit a sick relative in the last throes. Joliclerc politely answered in the negative. Mister Valdo had better stay where he was. They finally left him and Averil playing gin-rummy.

The caravan was stored in a garage opposite the town hall. Littlejohn was surprised when he saw it. If Waldo wasn't up to much in the way of brains, he was certainly good with his hands. The caravan was a beauty.

Plate-glass panels in the door, then a vestibule. Two doors from the vestibule each leading to a bunk-room, with two comfortable bunks apiece, like second-class compartments on the Wagons-Lits. Beyond, the living-room, like a little lounge with a sort of built-in pew in which you could dine. Then, at the front, a little kitchen side-by-side with the diminutive bathroom which had so dumbfounded Joliclerc. There was a plentiful use of plastics in the construction, and glass, mirrors and carved wood about it. Electric light and running water... The lot!

Joliclerc wasn't busy with the bathroom now. He took Littlejohn into the bunkroom, obviously until recently occupied by Uncle George. His travelling slippers were still there, where he'd kicked them off, beside the bed. A nightshirt with an embroidered collar in a leather case with 'G.K.' embossed in gilt on the flap. Then, a travelling wardrobe and a small leather handbag. The latter had been opened and its contents carefully laid on the bed by the police. Littlejohn had a surprise. Waldo had said his uncle enjoyed good health. No wonder!

It was like the counter in a chemist's shop.

Bottles of capsules covering everything from low and high blood pressure down to chilblains and cramp. About five different patent medicines for dyspepsia, biliousness, food poisoning, migraine and sepsis. Various coloured powders and tablets; sleep producers, nerve soothers, pain killers...Bromides and bicarbonates, hypophosphates and hydrates, and a lot of anti-biotics bearing the labels of French pharmacists, who could supply them without prescriptions whilst their English colleagues weren't allowed. Uncle George must either have been a hypochondriac of the type which, given his own way, would have brought the N.H.S. down in ruins, or else he was a sort of unqualified quack anticipating a mob of eager patients.

'Samples of all these have been taken for examination...'

Someone was going to be busy!

'... As our medico-legal people said, poison could have been introduced in any of them and swallowed without his knowing. They're looking for arsenic among them. If they find it...well...'

Well what? Anybody could have introduced it, from the chemists who sold the medicines to the porters who carried the portable pharmacopoeia...Even Waldo or Averil...

Suddenly, a policeman broke in on them. He'd hurried so much that he had to rest a bit before he could regain his breath.

'They've found the body!'

'Whose?'

Joliclerc knew, but objected to half a tale.

'L'oncle Georges...'

They couldn't pronounce Keelagher properly at the police station, so now in the vernacular it was the Case of Uncle George.

'Where?'

'St. Raphaël.'

'They didn't get far, then.'

'The car wasn't there. Just the body.'

'What part of St. Raphaël?'

'Between St. Raphaël and Fréjus, near the new church, there's a large piece of land awaiting development. It was there. Just near the signboard which says *Défense de Déposer des Décombres.*'

Tip No Rubbish!

Poor Uncle George.

CHAPTER FOUR
THE WASTELAND

The body from the rubbish heap at St. Raphaël had been brought to the morgue at Cannes and lay there awaiting identification. In view of Waldo's nervous condition, it was thought better that James should do the job. A message to the consulate at Nice was hastily sent. James had been there for some time and the consul had been carrying on a polite but evasive argument with him. The diplomatic restraint of both parties was gradually wearing thin. James was beginning to threaten and use what he thought were his big guns; his own close friendships with members of the British cabinet and his uncle's importance in the City. The consul was relieved when the news came that James was wanted at once in Cannes.

'So, the body's been found!'

James seemed to regard it as a triumph.

'Now perhaps you'll change your mind and definitely pull some official wires and get us out of this mess.'

'I suggest you go to Cannes right away and see what has developed, Mr. Keelagher. We'll help all we can, but this may be the beginning of real difficulties. I ought to warn you of that. Keep in touch.'

'Real difficulties!'

James repeated it to himself over and over again all the way back. He was in for a shock when he got there.

'Is this a joke?' he asked when they showed him the body. 'This isn't my uncle. It's a tramp!'

It was, too!

The poor remains on the refrigerator slab were those of an ageing man, who looked as if he hadn't had a shave or a square meal for months. He wore tattered trousers held up by string, the striped worn-out remnants of what might once have been a yachtman's jersey, and an old coat several sizes too large for him. He had no socks and his once heavy boots had decomposed into what looked like a pair of aged sandals full of holes. It was the latter which had connected him with Uncle George Keelagher.

The dead vagrant had evidently possessed some rudimentary notions about finance. In one boot, he had hidden a wad of banknotes and in the other a thin book of English travellers' cheques drawn in favour of Mr. George Keelagher. The tramp must, somehow, have scented money in the cheques and had retained them in the best hiding-place he could think of.

'That isn't Uncle George.'

Joliclerc shrugged.

'We thought it wasn't, but we had to make sure.'

'And you brought me hell-for-leather back to Cannes for this? It's an outrage. I wonder what nonsense you'll be up to next.'

Littlejohn, interpreting, as usual, softened it off a bit.

James wished he'd been at home. He'd have made the police sit-up for this. He'd have gone to the Home Office about it.

Littlejohn and Dorange were together there. Dorange, anxious to release Littlejohn from his unhappy predicament, had decided to take a hand personally and sort out matters as soon as possible.

How had the vagabond got hold of Uncle George's money?

He hadn't died of arsenic poisoning, either. Somebody had stabbed him in the back.

It was assumed that somewhere or other he'd come across George Keelagher's body, gone through the pockets, taken the valuables, and then left it where he'd found it. Flush with funds, he'd probably started to flash his money about and excited the attention of someone who determined to share it. The tramp's body had been stripped of its possessions, too. No papers, no money, except that hidden in the toes of his oversized boots. Nothing except that to link him with Uncle George.

Now, the routine of finding where the tramp had lately been prowling would have to be started.

One thing about the new discovery was that it confirmed Waldo's story and seemed to create a definite link with the body of Uncle George, wherever that might be.

The tramp obviously hadn't stolen the car from the park at Cannes. He wasn't the type to drive any kind of car, to say nothing of a stolen one. The car thieves, somewhere in their flight, had discovered the cargo they were carrying and had cast it out as soon as they could.

The town police of Cannes were not long in identifying the body in the morgue. It was that of a regular, who haunted the Coast, scratched together a living on the quaysides, slept either in gaol or in the open, and had actually been seen by one of the local officers making-off in the direction of St. Raphaël the day before. He must have been hurrying, too, for he had crossed the Estérel, all twenty-five miles of it, in the course of a day. Perhaps he'd managed to thumb a lift on the way.

Somewhere between Cannes and St. Raphaël, therefore, it was likely that the body of George Keelagher had been ditched. The police couldn't have chosen a worse area to search.

Word was passed on to experienced men of the district. Country policemen, gardes champêtres, gamekeepers, forest wardens gathered west of Mandelieu for an organised search of the Estérel. By no means an easy job.

The savage mass of the Estérel thrusts itself from the mountains down to the sea between St. Raphaël and Cannes. A huge wilderness of vivid coloured porphyry, blue and green rock which changes colours under the sun to yellows, violets and greys. Part of it is *garrigue,* rocky uncultivated wasteland covered in prickly oaks. Other areas are covered in dark green pines and luxurious vegetation which tumbles down deep fissures. There is *maquis,* too; great areas of thorny bushes and impenetrable thickets, in which a man might lose himself and never be found. No tree at hand in the *maquis* with which to take one's bearings, supple shrubs pressing on every side and closing up again as soon as disturbed. Low, lush, mobile forest, fluid, like the sea, closely embracing the swimmer. *Le gros bois.* The great forest.

If Uncle George's body were hiding there, a poor chance of coming upon it.

The Keelaghers had camped near Les Adrets, almost the highest point between St. Raphaël and Cannes. A notorious spot for bandits at one time, sandwiched between the heights of Mont Vinaigre and the Massif du Tanneron. Perhaps it had suited the tastes of Uncle George, who had chosen the site for his last night's resting-place. It gave Littlejohn the shudders.

Dorange and Littlejohn joined the searchers at Les Adrets and the brigadier of the Cannes police, who had been there before on the matter of impounding Waldo's caravan, showed them the spot where the family had settled for the night. As camp sites go, it wasn't a bad one. Almost surrounded by trees and undergrowth, it was well protected from the wind and the curiosity of passers-by on the highway. It was within five minutes' walk of an inn in case any supplies ran out.

But the whole place had an ominous air about it. It was said the brigands and cut-throats had once haunted the neighbourhood. They seemed to have left an aura behind long after the law had wiped them out. There remained a vague feeling of menace. The same feeling which Littlejohn remembered pervading the fierce country of the Basses-Alpes, not very far away, where, at Digne, he had attended the Dominici trial as an observer. Once off the main route, teeming with tourists out for a good time, you felt everything was savage, ruthless and silent, watching your every move. Here it was that Uncle George had ordered Waldo to stop and pitch his tent for the night. Intent on his praying mantis, he'd ignored any danger of the place.

The police had been over the camping site with a fine-tooth comb. Nothing startling, except that someone had been sick nearby and the result had contained arsenic. Not much, but enough to arouse suspicions about Uncle George's death. A violent end, but more sophisticated than a casual prowler would mete out in a case of robbery with violence. Arsenic is an intimate weapon, fed to relatives, lovers, friends, whom you wish to get out of the way. That was why Waldo and his wife had been placed under restraint.

The searchers had now been marshalled, instructed, and sent off on their business. They vanished along side roads, lanes, goat-tracks and wood-paths. Some followed no charted course at all; others disappeared into the greenery of the *gros bois*. The ones assigned to the dangerous routes, the treacherous *maquis* into which it was folly to travel alone, went off in pairs.

Littlejohn and Dorange set out for the inn. *L'Auberge des Lentisques*. Almost inaccessible to motor traffic, it stood at the end of a half-mile track leading to the main road. From the front door, the passing vehicles could be faintly seen through the trees ahead; the back overlooked the vast Forest of Gallian. It was an inn in name only. Difficult to imagine anybody wishing to stay there. Better to sleep in the open. Even in winter or on a bad night, it would have been more savoury to shelter in a ditch in the fresh air. The place was tumbledown and flyblown and might have been a rendez-vous for murderers and smugglers.

The landlord matched the inn. A fat, unshaved little man with a large unkempt moustache, dressed in trousers and shirt. The waistband of the trousers bit so tightly into his flowing paunch that he didn't need braces or a belt. His eyebrows were bushy and almost hid his shifty eyes. He was sitting in the shade of a knotted old tree which grew in the dusty courtyard, in which a few scraggy fowl were picking for something they never seemed to find. Three men were passionately playing *pétanque* on the hard earth under the tree. Their steel bowls clashed viciously. They played slowly and carefully, as though all the world depended on it. There were four half-empty glasses of red wine on the rough table at the landlord's side.

The lot of them obviously knew Dorange. He mustn't have had anything against any of them for the time being, for they greeted him almost jocularly, but with the respect due to one who knew a thing or two.

'*Bonjour, M. le Commissaire…*'

One of the men, stripped to the waist yet wearing a disreputable beret, raised his headgear mockingly.

The landlord didn't speak or move, but spat in the dust. But he must have respected the little Inspector all the same, for he thrust two fat fingers in his mouth and whistled. A dark, sluttish girl, wearing felt slippers and with a low-cut frock and one breast almost bare, appeared and the landlord raised the same two fingers in a V sign. The girl returned with two glasses of red wine and put them on the table. Dorange sat on one of the old iron chairs and motioned Littlejohn to do the same. Then he took a drink of the wine.

'Same awful stuff!'

The landlord made a dreadful grimace supposed to be a friendly grin.

'Why bother to call then? It's all we have.'

'I'm here on business, Javert.'

The clicking of the *pétanque* bowls had ceased and now the players started to look uncomfortable. Dorange turned to them.

'You may as well all of you join in this little chat. Have any of you seen an Englishman wandering in these parts over the past two days?'

They all tried to look surprised. Most Englishmen passed *Les Lentisques* with great speed and if any of them halted for a look round, they always seemed in a hurry to get away again.

Some of the party shook their heads; others didn't even bother to reply. The landlord put the matter straight.

'None of them would know anything about what happened in the last few days. They've only arrived this morning. Two of them have been away nearly a week on a long-distance haul to Paris; the other's been working at a vineyard at Le Muy until today. Is it the old man whose body was swiped, along with the car it was in, at Cannes yesterday?'

'Who's been talking?'

'Things get around. The police were towing away the caravan and somebody overheard what they were saying. You ought to know that all the news is passed around here over a drink…'

'If there's anybody here to pass it around, yes.'

Dorange took out a gruesome photograph of the tramp found on the dump in St. Raphaël. It had been taken on the slab in the morgue.

'Now you're talking,' said the landlord, after he'd taken a good look at it. 'That's the one they called Belsunce. Nobody knew his name, but it was said he'd once been a priest. Which might be true. He wasn't born a vagabond. He spoke well. Is he dead?'

'That was taken on the slab of the morgue at St. Raphaël, so it's very likely.'

The landlord drank the last of his wine.

'Rest his soul! What happened?'

Dorange made a stabbing gesture.

'I'm asking you. Anything to say?'

'No! Who'd want to do-in a harmless old codger like Belsunce? He was here yesterday. And he'd money. Tried to be funny. Ordered Asti Spumante. He was out of luck.'

'Money. That's what caused it. Did he say anything?'

'Not a thing. He was in a hurry. Ate some bread and an egg, drank his wine, and was still chewing when he went off.'

'Which direction?'

'Fréjus.'

'As you're no doubt dying to know what it's all about, I'll tell you. Your Belsunce was found dead in St. Raphaël this morning. Stabbed. He was carrying quite a lot of money which had belonged to the Englishman I mentioned. We think the Englishman was killed near here. Have you seen any strangers about?'

'No. But Darluc, the forest warden did. He was here last night. He saw the old man twice on the night before he was missing. Once, he was on his hands and knees on the edge of the wood. Darluc said he thought he was saying his prayers, till he saw he was looking at something among the leaves with a magnifying glass. The second time he saw him, he was picking mushrooms on the edge of the forest.'

'Isn't Darluc with the search parties?'

'No. He's gone to Draguignan to see his brother who's in hospital there. He left early this morning.'

'When will he be back?'

'Late in the day.'

'I suppose he'll be calling here for a drink on the way home. Tell him to report right away at Cannes police station. Don't forget. Right away.'

'How's he to get there?'

'The way he got to Draguignan.'

'Motor-bike. He borrowed it.'

'He can borrow it again.'

They left them, Littlejohn still recovering from the effects of the foul wine. It tasted like turpentine.

When they returned to the main road, the traffic was thicker than ever. Everybody seemed to be hurrying to town before night fell. It wouldn't be much fun driving across the Estérel in the dark. Here and there they could see the members of the search party prodding the earth, examining likely places for the body, and occasionally someone blew a single blast on a whistle to mark the direction he'd taken. The orders were for three blasts if anything came to light.

'Shall we join them?'

Dorange, brisk and as fresh as a daisy, looked ready for anything. He was still wearing his light snakeskin shoes but was nevertheless prepared to face any kind of terrain.

'We might join the men in the *gros bois*?'

The forest was not far away, beginning with fringes of undergrowth which grew more and more impenetrable, and then the unrolling of the masses of trees, changing from deciduous in the shaded, moist, protected parts to firs and pines on the slopes facing the north.

They kept to the tracks used by the woodmen; it would have been folly to do anything else. Even then, the slim paths threatened at times to peter out. All along the way shrubs pressed on them. Scared birds and lizards fled as they approached. Except for the startled cries of birds, there was, for most of the time, complete silence and a sense of being embraced by something deadly. It would have been easy to grow panic-stricken; there was a primitive fear of the unknown in every step.

Now and then, someone would blow a blast on a whistle or a horn to signal his position to the nearby searchers. This was a cheerful, comforting noise and the answering blasts from other parts of the forest sounded like the tuning-up of a tin-whistle orchestra.

Dorange, who seemed familiar with the technique of such searches, was using a small compass to maintain his bearings.

'You seem familiar with these places, Jérôme. I must say they scare me. I wouldn't like to be lost here.'

'You'd probably never be found if you got off the beaten tracks. I spent two years here with the Maquis during the war, you know. I am familiar with the forests, but nobody but a fool would say he knew all about them. Some of us took temporary shelter here, but given a choice between the deepest parts of the forest and the Germans, most of us would have preferred the Germans. The heart of the-*gros bois* is terrible and drives most men mad. We decided it would be better to take to the hills...'

Suddenly, there was a signal – three blasts on the whistle – from quite nearby. There was a dead silence for a minute as though the rest of the searchers were mentally digesting the meaning. Then, answering calls from all over the place.

Littlejohn and Dorange did not make straight for the point of signal. Dorange led the way again to the next junction of the forest paths and, after consulting his compass, struck off along another track. The woodman who had given the alarm continued now and then to repeat it. The posse of searchers slowly converged on the place. The journey seemed interminable to Littlejohn. He was dripping with sweat and exhausted by the heavy moist heat. Walking was difficult, too, although to see the sprightly springing movements of Dorange, you wouldn't have thought so. It was unwise to smoke in what seemed to be a huge tinder-box and where the very mention of matches, sparks and fire was enough to cause a riot among the natives. Later, the Superintendent was surprised to find out that they had actually covered less than a mile in the brush.

As they drew nearer the spot, they could hear the voices of other members of the party on their ways to the scene of the alarm. Suddenly, they were there. The fluent shrubs thinned out and parted and they were in a small clearing made by the felling of one or two large trees. A knot of men, police and woodmen, were standing around a body lying under a thicket. Nobody had yet disturbed it, but it was that of a man and he was quite dead. Nobody said much. They seemed dampened and depressed by the forest and what they had just found in it.

One of the policemen told Littlejohn that the clearing was a mere fifty yards from the open, if that.

'We must have just skirted it on our way out, Martel and me. We were returning when we came upon the body...'

It was obvious from the position of the dead man that he hadn't died where he lay. Someone had tucked him under the bush and shovelled some dead leaves over him to get him out of the way. Probably Belsunce, the vagabond, had found him in the open, taken the money from the pockets, and then dragged it into the woods to hide it. The longer the delay in finding the dead man, if he *was* found, the farther the tramp could leave it behind him. Only someone had killed the tramp, as well.

One of the gendarmes from St. Raphaël, a latecomer, was already telling the rest that the murderer of Belsunce had been caught.

'It was Ardoino, the man with the wooden leg. He tried to change a thousand franc note at a bistro on the quay and the landlord tipped-off a policeman. They took Ardoino in and found he'd a lot of notes he must have found in Belsunce's pockets, some of them of the same series as those they found in Belsunce's boots. Those were all new notes, you see...'

Trust Uncle George. Only the best for him!

The body was that of Uncle George. Before they moved it, Littlejohn recognised it. Waldo had said his uncle despised holiday clothes as childish. On holidays, he dressed just as he did when he went to the City. Not even a soft collar. James must have inherited the idea. He, too, had travelled to the Riviera dressed like a counterjumper. Uncle

George had been wearing a good dark suit when he met his death. His linen was starched and white; his tie modest and neatly knotted. He looked smart for his funeral march in spite of what he'd gone through. He even wore a gold ring on his little finger and his watch was in its proper pocket. The priestly Belsunce had obviously a technique of his own. In spite of his poverty, he'd a respect for the dead. He'd only pinched the cash, which, as his former theological studies had doubtless taught him, was of no further use to Uncle George, now with God. So, we hope, was the renegade Belsunce, in spite of his apostasy.

The gendarme from St. Raphaël was still telling his tale. He wanted everybody to think the police of the Var department were more efficient than those of the Alpes Maritimes.

'... Our fellows were soon on the ball. In a couple of hours we'd combed all the low pubs and sure enough, Belsunce had been to one of them and started flashing his money about. He began cautiously, but as he got more and more wine in him he spent hundred franc notes instead of tenners, and then he pulled out one for a thousand. Finally, he got tight properly and started talking about his sins. He left saying he was going to find a priest and set himself on the right path again. He always did when he was drunk. Ardoino was in the same pub and was as good as tight when he left, too, just after Belsunce. He must have followed him and tried a bit of robbery with violence that was a bit too violent... It's an open and shut case. We're on our toes at St. Raphaël, I can tell you...'

A little man in what looked like a boiler suit and almost overwhelmed by an enormous walkie-talkie apparatus, had been keeping in touch with a police car on the highroad, from which the search was controlled. He soon got busy telling his contact what had happened in a yapping, excited voice. His report quickly brought a doctor, who was followed by the officials of the enquiry, the *parquet,* from Cannes. They proceeded to measure everything, hunt for clues, take photographs, whilst the doctor examined the body.

The cause of death was obvious, and it wasn't arsenic. Uncle George had been killed by a bullet through the chest. It was a clean job, it turned out later. In at the front, through the left ventricle, and out at the back. Very little blood had escaped. The doctor provisionally guessed at a shot from a few feet away from a revolver. Later, the experts said it must have been an old type of weapon. It might have been easy for Waldo and Averil to miss the cause of death in their bemused state and hurry to get the old man wrapped-up and away. That might be cleared-up in further questioning.

Belsunce had merely taken Uncle George's money. His watch, ring, and other valuable odds and ends, such as a gold tooth-pick, were still in their places, as was his wallet, minus banknotes, carefully replaced. Among such objects was found a silver box, a little smaller than a snuff-box. It contained a white powder which might have been saccharine or even cocaine. It was neither. The police surgeon examined it and even gingerly tasted it from the tip of his cigarette-stained finger.

'Subject to appropriate precise tests, I'd guess this is arsenic. The oxide...'

He'd been told about the arsenic found in the vomit on the site of the crime.

It looked as if Uncle George had been trying to poison himself or someone else. An autopsy would help to clear that up. Or, with his mania for self-medication, he might have been trying to cure himself or improve his health by using arsenic, a known tonic in small doses.

The picture of the past twenty-four hours thus began to unfold itself.

Uncle George's early rising and assassination. The discovery of his body outside the caravan by Waldo and Averil, who thought he'd died of a heart attack brought on by a surfeit of mushrooms. The hasty rush to Cannes in the car, with the body wrapped-up in a blanket in the back seat. The theft of the car and the apparent discovery of the gruesome cargo in the back by the thieves, who'd jettisoned it on the Estérel in a quiet spot not far from the scene of the earlier crime. The ex-priest, Belsunce, having stumbled across the body, stripped it merely of cash and went off and got drunk in St. Raphaël. Then, Ardoino, finding him flush with money and killing him.

The spectacular events since Uncle George's arrival on the Estérel had made almost everybody forget what started it all. The murder of Uncle George. That was it. And somewhere his murderer was likely to be fogotten in the dramatic and exciting trappings of the crime.

After all the commotion and the horrible excursion into the *gros bois,* it felt almost refreshing to Littlejohn to think about Uncle George, alive and a nuisance to his family. He wanted to know more about him. When he got back to the police station in Cannes, he put through a call to Scotland Yard, and asked for his colleague Inspector Cromwell. Cromwell's promotion had altered none of their happy partnership, but Cromwell was distressed when he heard about his Cousin Waldo.

'I'd be glad if you'd keep an eye on him, sir, and befriend him. He had a bad time in the war.'

'I'm doing my best, old chap. Now, I want you to do something for me ...'

And he gave him a lot of details about obtaining the parts of the jigsaw which, when assembled, would bring Uncle George to life again.

Chapter Five
'Pontresina'

M iss lucy Keelagher was taking tea when Cromwell arrived. The news of her brother's death had reached her, but she seemed quite unmoved. She was fond of hot muffins for tea and nothing was going to prevent her daily enjoyment of them. Not even the thought of George, which she put aside.

She had attached to the main gate with drawing-pins a postcard written in her firm Victorian handwriting.

NO REPORTERS ADMITTED.
TRESPASSERS WILL BE PROSECUTED.

There was a small crowd of newspaper men and other would-be intruders outside, but none, as yet, had dared to violate the privacy of Miss Keelagher. When Cromwell arrived they surrounded him.

'You the police?'

'What makes you think that? I'm a relative.'

The reporter removed his hat and offered his condolences, for which Cromwell thanked him, but closed the gate between them.

'Have a muffin and a cup of tea,' said Miss Lucy after Cromwell had tendered his sympathy and presented his family credentials proving his distant relationship with Waldo.

'I never thought much of the Bicester Keelaghers, but you seem a nice young man. And I'd no idea we'd the police in the family. That's a great comfort. It will make matters easier. Since last night, when the news of my brother George's sorry escapade in France arrived, the house has been surrounded by newspaper interviewers. I think some of them must have camped in the garden overnight. They are very nice men, but I cannot *do* with them. They upset my routine. Your being a relative will make things much better.'

It would, too! But perhaps not in the way Miss Lucy was meaning.

She was rather a hard case, thought Cromwell. She looked to have been immured in *Pontresina* since Edwardian days. *Pontresina,* by the way, was the name of the house, commemorating an ecstatic honeymoon in Switzerland by a long dead Keelagher who was later divorced. Miss Lucy wore a heavy baggy jumper she'd knitted herself in lavender wool, and a tweed skirt which she might have constructed herself, too, from the folk-weave a friend had made on a machine in her attic. It was longer at the back than the front and gave her the appearance of being slightly out of plumb.

'More muffins, please,' she said to the German maid, who was serving with her for a year to learn English language and ways and was getting her money's worth, too.

The feast was in the nature of a rite. The squelching of hot butter and the smacking of lips, and Miss Lucy was deaf and dumb conversationally until it was over. Cromwell, whose liver bothered him now and then – a defect inherited from his father – was sure he was in for a bilous attack, but was prepared to risk it in the line of duty. After they had both mopped-up and Cromwell had wheeled away the tray, Miss Lucy intimated that she was ready for a cosy talk.

She was small and thin, with bright black eyes, a beaked nose, tight lips and a mass of grey hair reared on the top of her head in an old-time fashion, which, with a few added wild adjustments, had just become the vogue among beatnik young ladies. Her complexion was pink and netted with wrinkles and her hands were small, graceful and white. She wore a lot of jewellery – bangles, chains, rings and brooches – which jangled when she toddled about.

'Is it true my brother was shot to death?'

She said it without a shudder. Her entire reading consisted of devotional works morning and evening and crime stories during the day. She read a thriller a day from a library where they called her *Old Bloodthirsty.*

'Yes, I'm sorry to say.'

'I'm not a bit surprised. It's a wonder somebody didn't do it before. He was a most difficult – one would almost say, objectionable man.'

Cromwell must have looked reproachful.

'I daresay, Oscar...You did say your name was Oscar, didn't you...?'

'Robert, Miss Lucy.'

'Robert, then. I daresay, Robert, you must think I'm terribly callous talking like this, but it is a great relief to me to have the house to myself at last after years and years of bickering and bullying. Of course, when one of the family dies, one naturally mourns them, if only formally. As you are a relative, I can tell you frankly, that I shall shed no tears. He was a nasty little boy and grew up into a nasty little man. In his childhood, he used to catch flies and put them in cages made of pins and corks just to torture them, and in his last years, he played about with those horrible mantis things and watched them gobbling each other up. As soon as I heard of his death, I put them all in the greenhouse boiler...'

It looked like going on for ever. Cromwell tried to dam the flood.

'You weren't good friends, then?'

'No, Robert, we were not. For the past fifteen years we have occupied separate parts of the house and communicated, when necessary, by notes pushed under doors. His wife ran away with another stockbroker many many years ago. He then came and established himself here, much against my wishes. The house is mine now, but whilst George lived, it was a part of a trust in which we both shared. He was bitter and vindictive after his wife fled and a nuisance to the rest of the family. I wouldn't have been surprised if Waldo or James had stabbed him to death long before this...'

She looked around at the heavy Victorian furniture, the thrillers in great numbers on shelves on the walls, and the roaring fire (in August!) and sighed.

'It's nice to get a bit of peace in one's declining years.'

If she hadn't been so elderly and frail and thus an impossible suspect, she might have been added to the list of possible murderers of Great-Uncle George!

Cromwell decided to give Miss Lucy another thrill.

'There is another strange thing in the case, Miss Lucy. Although your brother died of a bullet in the heart, the autopsy revealed, as well, the presence of arsenic in the body. Not enough to kill him, but a suspicious amount. You will doubtless know that arsenic is often administered in instalments, so to speak, by poisoners. Its effect is cumulative...'

He knew he wasn't telling her anything she didn't know. In addition to the crime fiction on the shelves, there were volumes on famous trials, encyclopaedias of murder, case-books, and dictionaries of crime.

'Yes, yes. That's right!'

She was breathlessly excited.

'When the body was found, there was, in the vest pocket, a small box containing a white powder. The French police had it analysed and it turned out to be arsenic oxide. We wondered if the box were your brother's or if he picked it up somewhere and put it in his pocket...'

Miss Lucy didn't allow him to complete the tale.

'Of course it was George's. That explains quite a lot.'

She sat back in her large armchair and looked very pleased with the information. It must have solved a puzzle in her mind.

'I now speak to you as a relative, not as a policeman, Robert. Although George and I lived completely separate existences, I always kept an eye on him and followed what he was doing. One never knew what he would be up-to next and, after all, I had my own interests to watch...'

She looked quite capable of doing it, too, in spite of her age.

'I therefore, unknown to him, kept a key to his study and also to his secretaire. The secretaire was my father's before it was George's, and I knew where to find the spare key when I needed it. It was not idle curiosity which prompted this, but self-defence. I used to look through his desk and papers now and then when he was away. I'm sure you'll understand, Robert. You seem to be an understanding man.'

Cromwell nodded and looked as sympathetic as he could.

'One day when I made one of my periodic inspections of the desk, I found a book on therapeutics open at the page on Arsenic. At first, I was very frightened. I thought perhaps

George was planning to poison *me*. He had motive for doing so, because he and I were beneficiaries under my father's trust and the death of one of us brought all the funds to the survivor for life. George was a greedy man ... Excuse me, I'll see if I can find the book I mentioned ...'

She hastily left the room, after taking a small bunch of keys tied together with tape from the drawer of her own desk.

Cromwell looked absently around the room again. There was a gothic touch about it. Old-fashioned, eccentric furniture. The sort of place where mad people lived and tried to do-away with one another, stealthily!

Great-Uncle George had, to say the least of it, been a queer card. Miss Lucy seemed as bad, if not worse. She gave one the impression of hating her brother so much for some reason or other, which for years had almost dominated the whole of her thoughts. It had nearly driven her round the bend. He wondered what great wrong Uncle George had done to his sister.

She was back with a large medical book, already open at the heading *Arsenic*. Before she handed it to Cromwell, she thought she ought to explain.

'George was a hypochondriac. His study is lined with medical books, quack theses, herbals, cures and systems of one kind and another. He was a sickly child, always being given either cough mixtures, cold cures, purges, brimstone and treacle, iron pills, or something else for his many ailments. It paved the way for self-medication. As he grew older, George spent a lot of his spare time diagnosing his imaginary ailments and treating them with one thing or another. Now and then, in a panic, he would go to the doctor, but having sought advice, he never took it. You see, as in everything else, George knew best and certainly better than the doctor. He was afraid of death, terrified of help-lessness or senility, dreaded losing his vitality of mind and body and having to give-in to younger men. So, like the old alchemists, much of whose works he studied, he sought some kind of elixir of life. He was always dosing himself with one specific or another. Arsenic was his latest. Look at the paragraphs he has lightly marked in pencil...'

Cromwell was bewildered. He wondered what was coming next. Give him a crook or a tough and he knew what to do. Crackpots, however, were outside his field of action. He wished Littlejohn were with him.

The arsenic eaters of the Tyrol can take as much as six grains of white arsenic every two days. It strengthens the muscles and the breathing, imparts a sense of great invigoration and enables them to carry enormous loads up almost perpendicular mountains...

It looked as if Uncle George had been trying the arsenic cure for old age! Increasing his health and vigour, enabling him to carry enormous burdens, like a young, strong man. He must have been giving himself small doses, perhaps by way of a start, for the autopsy had not revealed any great quantity of the drug.

The text-book mentioned that one of the effects of arsenic was to cause the taker to grow stout. Uncle George was reported to have been lately putting on weight and looking much better for it.

'That would seem to explain George's carrying arsenic. He was dosing himself with it. Yet another of his silly ideas...'

At least, this seemed to eliminate the arsenic feature and leave the way clear for tackling the shooting. Cromwell made a note of it in his black notebook and finally snapped the elastic band back in place.

'Had Mr. Keelagher any enemies?'

He knew it was a rather stupid question. It was opening the way for further denunciations by Aunt Lucy.

'Yes. As you have gathered, I am perhaps enemy number one. But, on no account would I have taken his life. It would have been entirely against my principles. I believe in a Higher Power who metes out retribution to the unjust. I have had many examples in the case of my brother. In his selfishness, he always feared he might, in old age, find himself without anybody to take care of him. He could not bear the idea of my getting married. He wished to keep me in reserve for his own purposes, to make me a kind of housekeeper and nurse, in pickle, in case of need. But for George, I could have married. I had many offers. One, in particular, which took away all my real happiness when George intervened and prevented it. The man – my dear Herbert, I have never forgotten him – was forced to give up all idea of marriage for he got himself in financial difficulties. I had no proof that it was George's doing, but I knew. Justice was administered to my brother in full measure. His wife, whom he adored, mainly because she was very rich, ran away with one of his partners, the man whom he most trusted...'

Cromwell listened bemused. How much was true, and how much the imagination of a lonely disordered mind?

'His other enemies?'

'He must have had quite a lot in business. He was a ruthless man and not averse even to taking a rise out of those he called his friends. I remember one, who was ruined through a speculation which my brother had recommended, swore to shoot George on sight. But, unhappily he shot himself instead. There must have been many like that...'

Cromwell realised that there was little use in pursuing the matter further. To take lists of Uncle George's enemies from Miss Lucy would bring in a motley crew, most of them probably born in her imagination. Already, from the conversation now progressing, she was growing very excited. Her eyes shone, her lips were tight with hatred and relish, and she looked ready to indulge in an indefinite session of washing Uncle George's dirty linen. Cromwell was turning over in his mind the best way of gracefully backing-out of the interview, when an interruption occurred by the entrance of a servant.

It was not the German girl, learning heaven knew what of English language and ways from Aunt Lucy, but an elderly woman, an obvious housekeeper, who had, under cover of collecting the cold and empty muffin dishes, arrived to see that all was well with Miss Lucy.

'Well, Miss Lucy, and have you had an enjoyable afternoon? You mustn't tire yourself, you know. The strain of what has happened will be too much for you if you don't take a rest now...'

The newcomer turned to Cromwell. She was a waxen-faced, powerful, white-haired woman of fifty-odd, evidently, from the way she addressed Miss Keelagher, an old retainer. She smiled at Cromwell, who must have had his card marked as a member of the family beforehand.

'She's not been well and mustn't overdo it, you know, Inspector Cromwell. It was nice of you to call and it's taken her mind off her troubles...'

She turned again to her mistress. Miss Lucy gave her an innocent look, as though the conversation had been a religious one, instead of murderous.

'But now we've got to go to bed for our lie down, haven't we, Miss Lucy? Then we'll be able to enjoy our dinner...'

She spoke to her like a child. Miss Lucy obviously enjoyed it. She behaved like a child.

'I'm very tired, Benson. I'll be glad to rest. Robert must call again very soon and have a talk with me. I've enjoyed it very much.'

You would have thought butter wouldn't melt in Miss Lucy's mouth. Only five minutes before, she'd been enjoying the idea of shooting her brother!

Benson led her away after Cromwell and Aunt Lucy had shaken hands. She even kissed Cromwell because he was a relative. With the exception of Uncle George, who strongly disapproved of it, the Keelaghers were a great family of kissers. They'd have thought something was gravely wrong in the family if their comings and goings were not sealed by greeting and farewell kisses. Nobody minded Uncle George's objections. Nobody ever wanted to kiss him in any case.

As Aunt Lucy tottered out of the room, leaving Cromwell almost forgotten in her eagerness to take a little nap before her big evening meal, he managed to whisper a word or two to Mrs. Benson.

'If I wait here until you're free, could you spare me a minute or two? There are one or two things I don't want to tire Aunt Lucy with ...'

He underlined *Aunt Lucy.* Coming on top of the kiss, it confirmed the family connection and made the housekeeper only too glad to oblige.

'Of course ... Ten minutes ...'

Mrs. Benson returned to Cromwell in less than ten minutes. The excitement of a visitor who had stayed so long with her had tired Aunt Lucy and she had fallen quickly asleep without the usual fussing and chatter.

'She seemed very excited after her conversation with you, Mr. Cromwell. Have you been talking about poor Mr. George?'

'Yes. She doesn't seem greatly upset about his tragic death. In fact, she seems to be looking forward to a more peaceful existence in the future.'

'They never got on well. She resented his coming to live here right from the beginning. He, in turn, was very impatient with her. In his time, Mr. George was a clever man. He still was when he died, but he'd developed cranky notions about his health and, if I may say so, talked a lot of nonsense about it. He was too preoccupied with illness. Miss Lucy wasn't very clever. She spent a lot of time reading detective stories, which Mr. George despised. Why shouldn't she read them? They passed the time away and entertained her.'

The housekeeper seemed a sensible, intelligent woman. Cromwell thought she might be of help. He asked her if Miss Lucy really hated her brother.

'I wouldn't say that. Not really, although she heartily disliked him. He used to bully her a bit and, you must remember, he liked his own way and took-on when he didn't get it. What has she been saying to you?'

'She talked about his preventing her from getting married and treating the rest of his family badly. She seemed to think that there could be quite a long list of candidates who might have murdered Mr. Keelagher.'

'Poor thing. She's got obsessions. She spends a lot of time alone and broods a lot on imaginary injuries. She's told me about Mr. George interfering between her and the man she was going to marry. Did she say his name was Herbert?'

'That's right.'

'Not long ago, it was Arthur, and before that, Richard. I wasn't here at the time she said all this happened, but I'd imagine it's a little game she plays with herself to while the time away. I don't suppose Mr. George cared whether she married or not.'

'I don't assume you'd know whether or not Mr. George made a new will lately…'

It was a routine question which Cromwell would have asked Miss Lucy if she hadn't suddenly decided she'd talked enough.

Mrs. Benson had an answer. She smiled in rather a superior way, as though proud of what she knew.

'It's funny you should ask that. He was going to make a new will. I know because he asked me and Richley to be witnesses when the solicitor called here for his signature to it. The lawyer is a man called Craddock. Richley and I stayed in one evening because he was due to call, but Mr. George put it off for a few days, because he decided to go to France with Mr. Waldo and his wife.'

'Did Mr. George get on well with his family?'

'No. He was always complaining about Mr. James neglecting him. He thought Mr. James was too preoccupied with his business and ought to call here and entertain his uncle more. He said he ignored him and showed no respect. As for Mr. Waldo. He's a very nice gentleman, but Mr. George objected to his wife. You see, Mrs. Waldo was a typist in the firm of which Mr. George was head. Mr. George said she'd set her cap at Mr. Waldo and compromised him so that he had to marry her. He said Mr. Waldo had married beneath him. Which was quite wrong. Mrs. Waldo is a very nice young woman. I think Mr. George found that out, too, later on. At first, he forbade them the house, but later they started to come…'

'And then he decided to go on his holidays with them?'

'Yes. I was very glad to hear it, but it was done with a purpose I think.'

'What purpose?'

'As I said, Mr. George had talked about a new will. In my opinion, and it *is* an opinion and not something I know for certain, Mr. George wanted to get to know Mr. Waldo and his wife better, so that he could make up his mind how to treat them in his will. After all, Mr. Waldo and Mr. James were his only close relations. They'd a right to expect him to remember them well in any will he made.'

'You don't know the details of what was in his mind about the new will or what might have been in any former one?'

'No. That's not my business, sir. I do know he used to get in terrible tempers about Mr. James neglecting him and about Mr. Waldo marrying a typist in the office who was only after his money. I once heard Mr. George say, in one of his tantrums, that he'd leave all his money to the dogs' home.'

'How did *you* get on with Mr. George, Mrs. Benson?'

'All right. I did my duty and kept out of his way when he was in one of his moods or tempers. Once or twice, he's given me the sack for something trivial he didn't approve of, but when I've told Miss Lucy that I was having to go, she's made it right again. She used to send Mr. George notes instead of talking to him.'

'How long have you been with them?'

'I was with Miss Lucy for about five years before Mr. George came to live here. His wife left him, you know. That was about twenty years ago. She was much younger than he was and, I believe, a bit flighty.'

'There are other relatives besides Mr. James and Mr. Waldo, I believe.'

'Yes. They're in Canada. Three cousins. Two were farmers, I believe, who've never kept in touch. The other, a much older man, was a monk. He called once when over here on a conference. I don't think Mr. George and he got on very well.

He certainly didn't stay the night here. He was dressed like a monk and was called Father Martin. Mr. George said he was a humbug, although to me, he was a very nice man. I think he put Mr. George out of countenance a bit, which was something fresh, I can tell you. Mr. George was very rude to him a time or two and used bad language purposely to annoy the priest, which it didn't, all the same. Mr. George wasn't in the habit of swearing and I'm sure he did it then to shock Father Martin. That's all the other close relatives I knew.'

'You mentioned a Mr. Richley, was it? Who's he?'

'Mr. Richley? He started as Mr. George's chauffeur, but as Mr. George and Miss Lucy hadn't enough to keep him busy driving them about, he became a sort of general man-servant about the house. They both used him and thought a lot of him.'

'Is he about the place now?'

'Yes…'

And somehow Cromwell was sure of it. He knew that someone was listening behind the door, and crossed the room quietly and flung it open.

He was right. Standing on the skin mat, head bent almost benevolently over a spot where the door had been, was a tall, heavy man, on whose face still glowed the approving smile with which he was listening to the conversation on the other side. He didn't seem surprised or guilty at being found eavesdropping. On the contrary, he straightened himself and gave Cromwell a deferential little bow.

'I'm sorry to interrupt the conversation, sir, but Mrs. Benson is wanted on the telephone. One of those reporters…'

Mrs. Benson excused herself and passed them to answer the 'phone, but Cromwell noticed that it was still in its cradle. She had to take it up and make-up a conversation to cover Richley's fib.

Chapter Six
In the City

The Stockbroking office of Keelagher & Heller was in Throgmorton Street and Cromwell found it a bit difficult getting hold of Mr. Heller when he called there. Equities had slumped, the Financial Times Index had fallen three points, and one of the huge banks had made a takeover bid for a rival. Even the foul death of Mr. George Keelagher had been relegated to the also-rans of financial news and Mr. Heller found the investigation of his murder a bore.

'Most inconvenient just now.'

'All the same, sir, this matter won't wait. I won't take up much of your time, but after all, it is a matter of murder.'

Had Cromwell been a substantial client, Mr. Heller would have offered him sherry and cigarettes. But he was only a policeman.

'I am willing to help you all I can, but what can I do? I'm as baffled as you are about poor Keelagher's death...'

Mr. Heller was a small, humourless man, dried-up like parchment...like a lizard. He had a lizard's bright eyes, too, watching all that went on, ready to bolt for shelter at the slightest sign of danger. He had succeeded George Keelagher as head of the firm on the latter's retreat into semi-retirement and was bitter because George had made a large fortune in his time by dashing speculation. Now, Mr. Heller was a very careful man and tried to choose prudently and reasonably. It didn't seem fair that the rash and impetuous one should always scoop the pool and leave the prudent one to gather the leavings every time. It wasn't good enough.

'I suppose you're interested in the late Mr. Keelagher's private finances. Well, let me tell you right away that I can't divulge any of his business to the police. It would be all wrong...'

'I was mainly trying to find out if you knew anyone likely to murder Mr. Keelagher. Had he any enemies?'

Mr. Heller looked almost scared to death and ready to run for cover.

'My *dear* sir! Are you asking me to level an accusation against my late partner or some person unknown who might have borne him a grudge? Because I can be of no help to you. I suggest you speak to Mr. James or Mr. Waldo. They are his kith and kin and could...'

'They've already been interviewed.'

This was going to be difficult. Like banging one's head against a stone wall. Cromwell began to brood on tactics, how to make the next approach.

Telephone.

Mr. Heller snatched the instrument and listened aggressively whilst someone was brought to the other end of the line. Then, his look softened. He actually smiled. A wintry folding of his features.

'Of course, I'll come right away. No, I'm not engaged. I'll come right over. Not at all. A pleasure...'

He gently laid the instrument in its cradle as though putting a sleeping baby to bed.

'I'm sorry. We'll have to postpone this interview. That was Sir Tostig Surtees, one of the government brokers, who wants to consult urgently with me. I'll have to go down to the Stock Exchange right away. Speak to my secretary on the way out and fix another time.'

Mr. Heller was like someone intoxicated by a stiff draught of patronage. He put on his hat, made for the door, hooked Cromwell on his arm on his way out, and deposited him in the corridor.

'Goooood morning...'

It all happened so quickly that Cromwell hadn't even time to ask where the secretary could be found. In any case, he wasn't going to be put off that way. He'd find another partner. He looked at the doors along the corridor.

Mr. Moon; Mr. Patterson; Mr. Heller; Mr. George Keelagher; General Office; Enquiries, ring and enter; Mr. Waldo Keelagher; and finally Mr. Smiles. Cromwell felt there ought to be a memorial wreath of evergreens or some such appropriate ornament hung on the door of the murdered man's room.

The name Smiles sounded good. It reminded Cromwell of the writer of the improving books he'd been forced to read when he was young. He knocked.

'Come in.'

Mr. Smiles was reading the Financial Times with his feet on his desk and a cup of coffee at his elbow. He looked up as Cromwell entered and gave him a welcoming smile, as though glad of someone to talk to. Cromwell got the impression that Mr. Smiles had been given the last and worst room along the corridor to keep him out of mischief.

'You from the Press?' asked Mr. Smiles, 'Because if you're here to ask my views on the effects of the Wall Street slump, I can't give you any. Half the market's on holiday, nobody's very much interested in investments just now, and equities decide to take a toss for no apparent reason. The Stock

Exchange is becoming more and more like a silly temperamental woman who doesn't know what she wants or why she does things. You can say that in your article. Sit down. I'll send for some coffee. But you've got the wrong man. My job's dealing with provincial clients. I'm busy in the afternoons. They get the news from the S.E. around eleven, talk it over with their friends at lunch, and then start ringing me up ...'

Cromwell came up for air after this spate of information.

'I'm from the police.'

Mr. Smiles looked a bit pained.

'Why didn't you say so at first?'

'You didn't give me much chance, sir, did you?'

'Not another tycoon gone phut, is it?'

'No. The death of Mr. G. Keelagher.'

'Ah ... That's got you guessing, hasn't it? But I've seen this coming.'

Mr. Smiles looked ready to start another talking marathon, and Cromwell thought it better to chip-in and control the conversation. He couldn't waste all day on one man who wouldn't talk and another who didn't know when to stop.

'Mind if I ask you a few questions?'

'Fire away. Here's your coffee. Do I know whodunit? Is that what you're after?'

Mr. Smiles was tall and heavy, like a rugby three-quarter gone to seed a bit, and he wore a dark handle-bar moustache, for he had been a fighter pilot in the war. He was the nephew of a peer and if four cousins who stood between him and his uncle died, Mr. Smiles himself might succeed to the title. Keelagher and Heller had taken him on as a junior partner because his uncle's portfolio, which they handled, was colossal.

'One has to be discreet about what goes on in one's firm. But you're the police, aren't you, a decent chap, and a model of discretion, I'm sure. Right?'

'Yes.'

'Well, old Keelagher and old Heller have been quarrelling like hell for weeks. You see, it was arranged in Spring that Keelagher should take it a bit easier. Heller was to become principal partner, and Keelagher sort of come in half-time. However, Keelagher wouldn't lay-off. Kept callin' in and chucking his weight about. And as Heller and Keelagher are about as different as chalk from cheese in the way of doing business, old Heller was getting peeved to death. They've had a row every day for the past month. Finally, Keelagher went off on his holidays to simmer down. Now, if this murder had occurred in England, I'd have said Heller did it. But as it happened in the South of France, he couldn't possibly... Couldn't have got there and back in time. He's been here bang on ten every morning whilst Keelagher's been absent. I'm sorry about that.'

Mr. Smiles cast a look of sympathy on Cromwell, as though upset at not managing to sew up the case for him.

'How did Mr. Keelagher and Mr. Heller come to start together? They seem an ill-assorted pair, if I may say so.'

'Old Keelagher, George's father, started the firm eighty years ago. Heller began here as a junior clerk and became a dealer on the Exchange. George Keelagher had no children to carry on and his nephews didn't take to stockbroking. James, his elder nephew, is in produce, pepper to be precise, and it suits him. His uncle never got on with him and didn't, I gather, fancy having him breathing down his neck as a partner. Waldo, the younger... very decent chap... was going in for law when war broke out. He was taken prisoner and it broke him up. When he came back, George Keelagher took him in here, although Waldo's not very bright.'

'So the firm is really run by you and Mr. Heller now?'

'Very nice of you to put it that way, old man. But you can count me out. I'm really here to look after my uncle Percy's investments and be nice to angry clients when their shares go down instead of up. Mr. Heller's the big shot now and I'll bet he's delighted that Keelagher's gone at last.'

There was a postcard propped against the inkpot on the desk and Mr. Smiles passed it over to Cromwell. It was a view of Aix-en-Provence.

'Waldo sent me that. Promised to keep me informed where their caravan rested so that I could forward their mail.'

The card was postmarked *Théoule* and dated the day before George Keelagher's death.

We are staying here in the wilderness above Cannes at a spot called Les Adrets. I will call at Cannes for any mail. Address to G.P.O. Poste Restante.
  Kind regards, W.K.

'Waldo's following in uncle's footsteps. Old Keelagher always kept us posted exactly where he was on his holidays, so that he didn't miss anything during his absence. Sometimes, he even 'phoned the office from distant places. He left the job to Waldo this time.'

'So you can't give me any views about this crime, Mr. Smiles? Why anybody should wish to kill Mr. Keelagher?'

'No. Hasn't it struck you that most likely some bandit or cut-throat caught old George early in the morning on his own and held him up for his money? Then, when he resisted, shot him. It was like the old chap to put up some resistance, you know. The only thing he seemed afraid of was being ill. He was a hypochondriac. When they come to tidy up his desk, they'll find enough patent medicines there to set-up a chemist's shop.'

'The bandit idea had struck the French police, but has more or less been rejected. Their theory, and it's well-based on the evidence, their theory is that Mr. Keelagher was shot for some motive other than theft. His murderer didn't even take his gold signet ring or watch away with him, to say nothing of his pocket-book. When Waldo and his wife took the body to Cannes in the car, the contents of the pockets seem to have been intact.'

Smiles laughed in spite of the tragedy.

'Wasn't it just like old Waldo to bundle-up the body and take it to the police, instead of bringing the police to the body? His mind was always full of queer scruples and uncertainties. And then to have the car and the body both pinched!'

'The car thieves got rid of the body very quickly. When they discovered what they'd got on the back seat, they jettisoned the corpse at the first lonely spot wide of Cannes. It happened to be very near where the crime was committed. There, a harmless old tramp, from all accounts, found it, and relieved the body of banknotes and travellers' cheques. He left the jewellery and the rest behind.'

'So it wasn't robbery with violence, then?'

'Not from all accounts. It seems, to a certain extent, to have been premeditated.'

Smiles ran his fingers through his hair.

'It baffles me. According to the papers, the old boy was found buried in about six inches of soil in a forest, wasn't he?'

'Not even buried. Just put under the nearest thicket where he couldn't be easily spotted.'

'What a way for anybody to have the curtain rung-down on him! Especially a man like old George, who thought so much about his dignity.'

'You mentioned quarrelling between Mr. George Keelagher and Mr. Heller. Was it just bad temper on the part of the pair of them because Mr. Keelagher wouldn't stay away in spite of being retired, and Heller wanted to be rid of him?'

'That's about it.'

'Anything more serious than that?'

Smiles hesitated.

'I guess there's no harm in telling you. Somebody else will if I don't. They were quarrelling about money.'

'Didn't they settle all that when George Keelagher decided to retire?'

'We all thought they had, but it seems arrangements were left over until George stopped doing half-time work and retired completely. I gathered that George asked what Heller thought far too much for his share of the goodwill. He contended that the firm owed its success to him alone and he'd created all the profits. Heller, on the other hand, insisted that George had done very well out of the firm when he was principal. Not only had he taken a good salary and drawings, but as senior partner he always saw to it that clients likely to give him hot tips were exclusively dealt with by himself. Old George made a packet out of speculating. Heller resented that. It all boiled down to Heller's jealousy.'

'I see. Nothing else useful to me, sir?'

'Not that I can think of just now. If anything turns up, I'll let you know.'

Cromwell said goodbye and thank-you and thoughtfully made his way to Wallbrook. There were the offices of Craddocks and Kings, George Keelagher's solicitors. Mr.

Mortimer Craddock dealt with the old man's business and Cromwell expected another rebuff there. Instead, he was well received. Mr. Craddock remembered him in connection with a confidence trickster who had twisted one of his clients and whom Cromwell had laid by the heels. Cromwell had met Mr. Craddock in court but never knew him by name.

'Well, Sergeant Cromwell...'

He expressed himself very gratified and congratulated Cromwell heartily when he was told that Cromwell was now an Inspector.

'This calls for a drink...'

And Mr. Craddock produced whisky and all that goes with it and drank the new Inspector's health.

'Very well deserved, too. What brings you to Wallbrook? Another confidence trick? I hear Flash Jim's in circulation again.'

Mr. Craddock was getting on in years, too. He must have been well over sixty and he carried his age well. He was tall, portly, almost completely bald, and he looked well-versed in the art of good living.

'I'm afraid it's much more complicated than Flash Jim this time, sir. It's about Mr. George Keelagher.'

It didn't seem to depress Mr. Craddock.

'Rest his soul.'

And refilled the glasses to drink to the peace of old George.

'The old boy's hit the headlines, what?'

Ironical, that after all his futile searching for the elixir of life, everybody referred to him as *Old*.

'Yes, and in spite of the newspaper theories that some bandit or other cut his throat for his money, the French police think there's more in it than that. There's a suspicion of deliberately planned murder about it.'

'Any suspects?'

'No. That's why I'm here. It's a matter of motive.'

'How can I help?'

He knew very well what Cromwell was after, for, in spite of his naïve look and his bonhomie, Mr. Craddock was a very crafty man.

'Did Mr. George leave a will which might give us an idea of the motive?'

Mr. Craddock bared his rather prominent teeth in a juicy grin.

'He did. He made it two days before he went on holiday. A very wise step. Always make your will before you leave for your holiday, Cromwell. You never know what will happen. Look at poor old George Keelagher.'

Cromwell downed the last of his whisky, just to give himself time to think out his next move.

'Without betraying professional confidences, sir, could you tell me if the will contained anything which might cause Mr. Keelagher's murder?'

Craddock was enjoying himself.

'I like the discreet way you make your point, Cromwell. There's something almost feline about it. I cannot allow you to see the will, or even recite to you its contents. Let's, however, put a theoretical case. If a man were making his will and had a sister who was very well-off herself and therefore made no provision whatever for her, you wouldn't say she'd any motive for murdering him would you? Except, of course, out of spite for being cut-out. Negligible, isn't it? Or if he had two nephews, his only near relatives ... Let's say one of them works in his business with him, and, instead of leaving him cash, he leaves him a share in the enterprise.

Not a motive for wishing to get the maker of the will out of the way, is it? As for the other nephew, he has by his own acumen in another line of business, made a fortune himself. If his uncle merely leaves him a few odds and ends of jewellery as mementos, *he* has no motive for killing his relative. Unless, of course, he's childish and just can't wait for his odds and ends. But we're dealing with so-called sane people, not lunatics...'

Mr. Craddock filled-up the glasses again. He was having a good time in his own way.

'The man making the will was once kindly disposed towards his servants. He'd formerly left a thousand, let us say, to his housekeeper and a similar sum to his manservant. If, when he made his new will, he retained the housekeeper's little nest-egg but struck out that of the manservant, whose loyalty he somehow doubted, neither has a motive. Murder for a paltry thousand? Not likely. Or murder for the *loss* of a paltry thousand...Well...perhaps in hot blood, but not after brooding and meditation. Not worth the candle. So, you see, nobody had any motive for killing our imaginary friend.'

Cromwell drank again. It was good whisky and made him feel a hundred per cent better in outlook and health.

'But sir...'

Mr. Craddock raised a large well-kept hand.

'Don't. I know what you're going to ask me. Where did our theoretical client dispose of his money? Reputed to be wealthy, he dealt with a mere thousand or so. Well, our friend had, let us say, a sense of humour. To agitate his expectant relatives he had, in times past when exasperated by them, threatened to leave the lot to the dogs' home. Naturally, the relatives were upset at first, but after repeated threats, the thing became a joke. They expected it every time the will was mentioned. They smiled knowingly. It was just the old boy's little game. All would be well when the will was read ...'

Mr. Craddock smacked his lips.

'When it is read, however, there is a surprise in store. We have said our friend had a sense of humour. Although he'll not be permitted to see the faces of the relations when the day comes, he liked to imagine them and chuckle over them. He *leaves* the residue to the dogs' home!'

Cromwell jumped.

'You mean to say, sir, that Mr. Keelagher ...'

'Inspector! Inspector! Didn't we agree to keep the little story in the imaginary category? Just to pass the time away over our drinks? *Please* don't materialise it and pin it on one of my oldest clients, who would be very annoyed if the contents of his will were published prematurely ...'

Cromwell nodded. He even laughed to himself.

'Of course, sir. Thank you for your funny story. I must tell that one to Superintendent Littlejohn when I see him. He'll enjoy that one. Dogs' home! That's a good one.'

But it seemed to cut out motive from the point of view of the will. Unless, of course, someone imagined he or she were going to scoop the pool and didn't know about the new will ...

In any case, one new point had come to light.

Mr. Keelagher's man-about-the-house, the lawyer's imaginary manservant, had been misbehaving and got himself cut-out. That might be worth following up.

Mr. Craddock bade Cromwell a hearty good-day and told him to call again whenever he was near Wallbrook. Cromwell made his way to the Underground. Another trip to *Pontresina* seemed appropriate.

CHAPTER SEVEN
'PONTRESINA' AGAIN

The Card prohibiting reporters was still pinned to the gatepost of *Pontresina,* but when Cromwell arrived there, Richley, the manservant, was prizing out the drawing-pins with a tin-opener.

He recognized Cromwell, and greeted him civilly. He seemed to think some explanation was due about his occupation.

'Miss Lucy pinned up this card, sir, and put in the drawing-pins with a hammer. Now, someone has written a rude word across it and I thought I'd better put-up a fresh one before Miss Lucy saw it.'

He finally succeeded in getting the card free and holding it by one corner like something diseased, he showed Cromwell the inscription in an illiterate hand.

Cromwell took the card without a smile, tore it in four, and thrust it down a street grid by the gate.

'Best place for that.'

'I h'intended to burn it,' said Richley, adding an aspirate in an effort to show his dignity.

'It didn't seem much good, did it, Mr. Richley? The reporters have got all they wanted from...was it the side gate?'

Cromwell didn't like Richley. He was fat and florid and there was a yellow tinge in his complexion which seemed to indicate liver trouble through drinking his employer's alcohol. Or, at least, that was Cromwell's theory.

'Were you calling on Miss Lucy again, sir?'

'Yes. But I'd first like a word with you. Shall we go inside? I see your friends the reporters have noticed my presence already and we can't talk with them breathing down our necks, can we?'

'I gather from your…may I call it sarcasm, sir?…your sarcasm, that you think I am responsible for the information printed in the daily press. I would like to say, sir, right away, that I did see them in the kitchen *and* by the side gate, as you surmise, sir. They are a decent lot of gentlemen and were only pursuing their legitimate business. If I hadn't told them what they asked, someone else would have done so, and probably added a lot of scandal to it, as well. I was only protecting the family good name.'

Richley stretched himself to his full height and gave Cromwell the almost pious look of a man who had done his duty.

'Shall we enter?'

The kitchen was large and modern. In fact, it was almost like a factory. It looked as if Mrs. Benson, Richley and whoever might be their underlings had merely to turn a switch and all the work was done by electrical gadgets. Washers-up, refuse grinding and disposing machines, mechanical polishers, a house telephone…All the staff, particularly Richley, needed to do was to switch on. There was a half-read newspaper on the table, which Richley removed in his stride, along with an empty coffee-cup.

Richley must have read Cromwell's thoughts.

'Miss Lucy has a weakness for gadgets, sir. Young sales-men are always persuading her to buy them. Most useful in these times when domestic help is almost impossible to come-by. Personally, I'm not mechanically minded ...'

That was obvious! Anybody who would use a tin-opener for taking-out drawing-pins ... Cromwell looked round for the electric can-opener, but it was missing.

'Shall we adjourn to my room, sir?'

His way of speaking annoyed Cromwell, too. He couldn't just say *go*. It had to be *adjourn*. And Richley had a habit of underlining some words heavily and spitting from the effort. Dodging the spray prevented Cromwell from concentrating on the business in hand.

'How long have you been with Miss Keelagher, Mr. Richley?'

'Excuse me, sir. I was really with Mr. George, although he and Miss Lucy shared in paying my remuneration. I came here with Mr. George almost twenty years ago, it must be. I'd then been in his employ for two years. It's a long time. I shall miss Mr. George.'

He pushed the tip of his little finger in the corner of his eye as though trying to stop his tears.

'An awkward man to get on with?'

'If one didn't know his ways, yes, sir. One got used to him, though. One must not speak ill of the dead, sir, must one?'

Richley didn't like Cromwell, either. That was obvious. The way he underlined *sir* was almost offensive.

'You were happy at your work, then?'

'Yes. I wasn't interfered with. If I did the job properly. And I've always done my best.'

'I'm sure you have ...'

They were getting nowhere and with Richley, Cromwell was sure he'd find no help.

'I won't disturb you, then. I'd like to see Miss Lucy, please.'

'I'll let her know you're here.'

He didn't invite Cromwell to a seat, although there were a few comfortable ones about. Richley's private room was furnished with all modern comforts. Even to a large television set and a whisky tantalus on the small sideboard. There were a few books about, too; crime stories mostly. Cromwell picked one up. *Lucy Keelagher* scrawled on the fly-leaf in her own hand. Richley evidently made free of his mistress's crime library, to say nothing of other things, as well.

Miss Lucy was in her own room. There were coffee and biscuits on a tray by her side and she was sitting in front of the fire reading a crime novel.

'Good morning, Cousin Robert...'

It gave Cromwell a bit of a shock at first, but he realised that he was one of the family now. He was relieved when he found he wasn't so far advanced as to participate in the introductory kissing ritual.

'This is a great pleasure. Have a cup of coffee?'

She poured it out without waiting for his answer.

'Is this a social and family call, Robert, or is it business again?'

'Both, Cousin Lucy.'

He might as well accept the accolade! It would make matters easier, although his position in the family tree was very shaky.

'I thought I'd told you all there was to tell yesterday. However, draw up a chair and tell me right away what's brought you here again...'

He sipped his drink. It was good. Made in a percolator from fresh coffee. Miss Lucy caught Cromwell's eye as he distantly examined the apparatus, set out on the table.

'I like good coffee and it's so easy to make nowadays with all these mechanical and electrical machines around. Once, it took hours. Roasting, grinding, heating the pot...'

'I see you've quite a lot of labour-saving gadgets in the kitchen, too.'

'Oh, those. That's Richley's department. He's an expert in labour-saving devices. Whenever there's something new on the market, one or another of those electrical young men calls and demonstrates it and Richley is captivated. Each new machine means less work for him and the staff. He needn't run away with the idea that I don't know how fond he is of taking his ease. But one cannot refuse these requests for further assistance nowadays. It is a form of blackmail. Richley knows we can't do very well without him now. His kind of servants are very hard to find. So, he levies toll in what you call gadgets.'

Richley had said it was Miss Lucy who was responsible. Cromwell wasn't surprised. The fellow was obviously a crafty liar and probably an extortioner, as well.

'I came to ask you, Cousin Lucy, if Mr. George recently made a new will.'

Miss Keelagher pretended to be shocked, but really it was her little joke.

'You've not been long received in the bosom of the family before you're asking where the money's going, have you?'

'This is purely in connection with the case. Otherwise, I wouldn't presume...'

'You needn't look so hurt, Robert. I was joking. Yes; George did make a new will. He made it the day before he left for France. He'd been fussing about it for some time, I know. I found scribblings on bits of paper in his desk, when I made my secret inspections of what the desk contained. Finally, I saw the copy of the one he'd signed and left with Craddock, his lawyer. It was very amusing. It will surprise the family when it's read...'

She drew a pad and pencil to her from the side table. It was probably the one on which, in the past, she'd communicated with her brother. She scribbled and passed the note across.

Please open the door. Richley has a habit of listening.

She was right. When Cromwell did as he was asked, there was Richley, bending benevolently with his ear almost to the panel. He wasn't in the least put-out.

'Excuse me, sir. I came for the coffee things.'

He solemnly walked past Cromwell, as though he were some irritating obstruction, gathered up the cups and the apparatus, and made his way out without another word.

Cromwell was furious.

'Richley.'

'Sir?'

'Don't come back.'

'I had no h'intention of doing so.'

The door closed. By now, Cromwell knew that the extra aspirate meant that Richley was moved, and he felt satisfied.

'You shouldn't have rebuked him like that, Cousin Robert, although it was most amusing. It will take him days to recover. He'll probably sulk and be on his dignity.'

'But he won't give notice, pack, and be off, will he?'

'I think not.'

'He's too good a job here. I wouldn't be surprised if he isn't fiddling the household accounts, as well. He looks that sort.'

'Not mine, I can assure you. I make him present his accounts every month and I check them with the tradesmen.

George owed me quite a lot for that. I couldn't check mine without checking his, too. We each paid half and one half of the accounts without the other was useless.'

'We were talking about the will, Cousin Lucy.'

'Yes.'

She paused. It was obvious she wanted to tell Cromwell what it contained. Not that he didn't know, but she wasn't aware of that. And she was wrestling with her scruples about divulging what she'd found out by stealth.

'Come close, Robert. Richley is quite capable of returning if he scents that confidential family matters are being discussed. And one can't keep bobbing up and down to find out if he's behind the door.'

Cromwell moved as asked and they got in a huddle.

'I'll tell you, if you'll not speak about it elsewhere ...'

She paused, ready for the surprise.

'George left all his money to charity.'

Cromwell pretended to be amazed.

'Not to the family?'

'I have enough and he knew it. He very much resented the family trust, which was untouchable until one or the other of us died. Then the survivor got the life interest of the deceased. Eventually it goes to Waldo and James. Of course, it could have been broken by consent of all parties, but I would never agree to that. It was my birthright and my dear father created it well knowing that George would, if he could, get at the money in advance. But it was tight. George tried a time or two, but I declined. Only a month ago, we had a long correspondence about it. I think I told you, last time you were here, I refused to speak to him after he came and imposed himself on me. He just came. Never a by-your-leave. So ... Where were we?'

'Mr. George was trying to break the trust.'

'And I refused. That's why his will doesn't even mention me. I'm sure that only dear Mr. Craddock prevented George adding in the will some execrable words about me. There was a legacy of a thousand pounds to Mrs. Benson. I heard him asking her to be at his disposal to sign the will. Had she witnessed it, she would have lost her legacy. I telephoned Craddock and asked him to see that she didn't.'

'And that is all?'

'He left a smallish part of his capital in his firm to Waldo and a box of family mourning-rings and what is left of the family jewellery to James. You won't believe me when I tell you that I discovered that George had actually sold a lot of the valuable family relics, such as gold rings, miniatures ... In fact all that went to him when it was divided between us. He sold them, leaving merely the pinchbeck stuff. James will have a surprise when he gets his inheritance!'

She cackled.

She took his arm in her fingers and squeezed it to emphasise her next point.

'This will doubtless please you, Robert ...'

She lowered her voice until he could hardly hear it.

'Richley doesn't get a cent. In a previous will he was down for a few thousands. In the new one, George cut him off. I will invite you to be present as a member of the family when the will is read. We must be together when Richley receives the news. He will probably then pack his bag. I shall be glad. If I have to do the work myself, I shall be glad. He was George's man and I can't very well give him notice yet.'

Cromwell had an idea that Richley might be at the door again, straining to hear what was going on. He felt like loudly intoning 'Richley doesn't get a cent, then?' but decided it wouldn't be quite the thing.

'Why has he been cut-off?'

'I don't know. There were no clues in George's desk about it. And, as far as I could find out, they were on the best of terms when George left for France. I have wondered if Richley had some hold over George which could only be broken by the death of one of them and George was only able to show his resentment after he'd passed over.'

'When did he make his former will which embodied a legacy for Richley?'

'A few years ago. So, his disapproval of Richley must have started after that.'

'Yes.'

'I wonder if Mrs. Benson could throw a little light on the cause of the trouble.'

Miss Lucy threw up her hands.

'Oh, dear. That would never do, I'm afraid.'

'I wasn't suggesting that *I* should question her. Perhaps you could discreetly find out, Cousin Lucy?'

'No. I wouldn't care to do that. You see, Benson and Richley are—how shall I put it...? They are as thick as thieves! In such cases, one finds housekeepers and male servants either hate each other like poison, or are very close friends. There seems to be no middle way. All or nothing. I'm not suggesting anything immoral is going on. Benson has been with me since she was almost a girl. George brought Richley with him. The silence between George and me has, of course, strengthened Richley's position here. The same has applied to Benson. They have become go-betweens. She has served me and Richley has served George, but not exclusively. We have both had service from the pair of them. And I'm sure they have pooled their experience and information and made the most of it. You understand.'

'I certainly do.'

'When or after the will has been read, there may be a chance of speaking to Benson and finding out about Richley and my brother. But poor George's body is in the hands of the French. I don't know what they're doing to him or when they will send him home and let him have decent burial. So, one can't do much about it, yet.'

'Do you know much about Richley?'

'You surely don't suspect Richley of doing away with George?'

'No; but we like to cover every angle, you know.'

'I don't know very much. George knew all about him. He has a brother who lives in Fulham. He visits him at week-ends quite often. He works for the gas-board. I've seen him once or twice. He runs a little car and has called for Richley now and then. He very much resembles Richley. Big and flabby. When the pair of them get in the little car, they seem to ooze out of the doors and windows, if you understand what I mean.'

'Yes, I do. Did Richley stay on here whilst Mr. George took his holidays?'

'Not as a rule. He took his holidays, too. But George was a very awkward man, as I've already said. In times past, he's come home in the evening and said he was going away for a fortnight or three weeks the day after. Richley hadn't made any arrangements and used to get very cross. He'd go and stay in Fulham then with his brother, who, like himself, is a bachelor and grows chrysanthemums, I believe. Benson has told me all this. I wouldn't even trouble to ask Richley. I dislike him intensely and will dispose of him as soon as possible.'

'Did he go on holidays this time, when Mr. George left for France?'

'Yes. George, as usual, told him the night before. He went to Fulham. Benson sent for him when the news of George's death arrived.'

'He came right away?'

'Oh, yes. Hot-foot. His manner had changed, too. He has grown more aggressive. Presumably because there is no George here any more to keep him in hand...'

The clock on the mantelpiece cleared its throat and started to chime hoarsely. Then it gathered itself together and began to strike the hour of noon. It was doubtless valuable, but decrepit, and kept it up interminably. It seemed to please Miss Lucy.

'Lunch time,' she said. 'Would you care to stay for lunch, Cousin Robert?'

Why not? Cromwell would have to forage about for a place in the neighbourhood for a few sandwiches and a glass of beer if he didn't stay with Cousin Lucy. Perhaps, too, something fresh about George and his doings would come out over the pork chops.

'I'd very much like to, if it won't be any trouble...'

'Ring the bell for Benson, then, and we'll tell her to set you a place. It's only cold Melton Mowbray pie and junket today, but I'm sure you'll enjoy it.'

Cromwell rang the bell at the side of the fireplace. Instead of Mrs. Benson, Richley appeared. He was very much on his dignity after his passage of arms with Cromwell. His heavy nose was in the air and he tried to look down it at Cromwell.

'Beg your pardon, Miss Keelagher, but Inspector Cromwell is wanted on the telephone.'

'Excuse me, Cousin Lucy.'

Richley led the way and haughtily indicated the instrument in the hall.

'They wouldn't say who it was and I don't know 'ow they knew you were here.'

Cromwell might have been a stray dog which had wandered in.

It was Scotland Yard to whom he'd reported that he was going to Great Missenden and where they'd find him.

'There's been a Mr. Heller, of Keelagher and Heller, in the City, asking for you. It's very urgent. Could you ring him back, sir?'

'I'll do that. Is that all?'

'He wouldn't give a message.'

Cromwell dialled the number they gave him, and asked for Mr. Heller.

The voice that came on sounded altogether different from the sharp bark Mr. Heller had used on Cromwell when last they met. It was chastened, almost horrified, like that of a broken man.

'I must see you at once, Inspector Cromwell. Something dreadful has happened. I cannot speak about it over the telephone. I'd be obliged if you'd come right away. I'll wait for you.'

'Very well, Mr. Heller. I'll be there a little after one.'

Goodbye to lunch with Cousin Lucy! Lucky if he got any lunch at all now.

The sun was shining outside and through an open door along the passage. In the middle of a rectangular patch of sunlight was a dark silhouette, like a figure in a shadow show. It was Richley, listening-in round the corner. He ought to have known better than that!

'You can come out now, Richley. I've finished...'

The manservant emerged with as much dignity as he could muster.

'I was waiting, sir, to lead you to the dining-room...'

Cromwell fished in his waistcoat pocket and produced a sixpence.

'I suppose you'll want to collect for the outgoing call.'

In his surprise, Richley took it, and Cromwell went off to make his apologies to Miss Lucy.

CHAPTER EIGHT
DIRTY WORK IN THE CITY

This Time, Mr. Heller was supported by Mr. Craddock, and he looked as if he needed it. Cromwell met them just after two o'clock and they gathered in Mr. Craddock's office, where the papers on his desk were held in place by little bottles filled with lead shot and there was a smell of good tobacco.

Mr. Heller hadn't had any lunch. He didn't feel like it. No appetite at all. Mr. Craddock, on the other hand, was smoking a cigar and around him hung the gentle aroma of port. He had dined well, as usual, and it was not his custom to deal with business much before three o'clock as a rule. But today's events called for a little relaxation of the rules.

'You tell him,' said Mr Heller by way of an opening. He looked more like a corpse than ever and his complexion was grey.

Mr. Craddock removed his cigar and looked carefully at the glowing end.

'Mr. Heller and I have been in conference about something which came to light this morning, Inspector. We think we ought to tell the police, as it might help them in their investigations. Mr. George Keelagher died almost penniless and, at the time of his death, was absconding with monies belonging to his firm.'

'But...'

'There's no *but* about it, my dear Inspector. That is the truth.'

It took Cromwell some time to grasp it. Mr. Heller looked as if he hadn't grasped it at all. He sagged in his chair and the only words he could seem to find were 'The Scoundrel' which he kept uttering like the passing bell.

'Now, Mr. Cromwell, I must insist that you and the police keep this matter utterly confidential until the news gets out in the ordinary way. If it's dropped like a bombshell it may cause a panic. As it is, only Mr. Heller, by putting his personal resources in the firm in place of those taken by Mr. Keelagher, will prevent the firm of Keelagher and Heller from being hammered on the Stock Exchange. Our only reason for taking you into our confidence is that, personally, I know you well and admire you. You will respect our wishes. Have I your word to keep this information dark until we deem it prudent to release it?'

'I shall, of course, have to report it to my superiors, particularly to Superintendent Littlejohn, who is in charge of the case. Subject to that, I can give you my word.'

'In that case, I will telephone Scotland Yard ... or better still, call to see the Commissioner, who's a friend of mine, and ask that the matter be treated confidentially.'

'The Scoundrel!'

Mr. Heller tore at his few thin hairs desperately. Mr. Craddock rose and offered him a glass of brandy.

'Drink that, Heller, and pull yourself together. It's not the end of the world, you know.'

'The Scoundrel!'

Heller raised his glass and drank as though toasting Uncle George magnanimously, in spite of what he'd done.

'Is there anything else you'd like to know, Cromwell?'

Anything else! Cromwell knew nothing, as yet, except that The Scoundrel had rifled the till of his firm and decamped to France in a caravan with Waldo.

'How did it happen?'

Mr. Heller must either have been drinking before and the last brandy had tipped the beam, or else he had a poor stomach for alcohol. He hiccupped and suddenly became voluble.

'The Scoundrel! All the time I was nursing the firm and taking care, he was speculating on risky ventures and losing his own money as well as the firm's. It's positively scandalous. He's been living on the fat of the land, chucking his money about as though he were a millionaire, bullying me and his other partners as though he owned all Throgmorton Street...And actually he's been almost penniless. Then, to crown the lot, he's made-off with twenty thousand pounds of the firm's resources. It's not good enough. Where is divine justice, where, I ask you...?"

And floored by lack of response to his problem of philosophy, he burst into tears.

Mr. Heller wasn't used to weeping. He was an ignorant amateur at showing his feelings or betraying any softness. He became convulsed and beat the desk in his frenzy.

Mr. Craddock gave him another glass of brandy, as though hoping he'd pass-out and leave them unembarrassed and in peace to continue their talk.

Mr. Heller calmed down, but was now indignant.

'And to get himself killed before he could be punished for it. It was just like him. He never suffered for his misdeeds... *and* they were many, I can tell you.'

Mr. Craddock thought he'd better take over and talk Mr. Heller out, if necessary.

'Briefly, that was the case. Keelagher seems to have lost his own fortune, which was substantial at one time, in gambling on the Stock Exchange...'

'A Broker! A member of the Stock Exchange! It's unthinkable! It's immoral! It's indecent!

'All right, Heller. I agree. But let me get on. Inspector Cromwell hasn't all day to waste. As I was saying, Cromwell, Keelagher died a poor man. Before he left for his holiday, he had spent weeks contending with Heller about the final amount he would require for his share in the firm. He wanted another twenty thousand pounds. Mr. Heller...'

'I refused! He'd had enough already! Too much, in fact...'

Mr. Craddock raised his voice. It was loud and fruity and Heller with his gulping squeak didn't stand a chance with it.

'... As I was saying, they'd been arguing for weeks...months, in fact...about it. Finally, Keelagher seems to have made up his mind to terminate the problem in an original way. As a partner, albeit a part-time principal at the time of his departure, he had authority to sign the firm's name on cheques. This he did before he went away. He drew a cheque for twenty thousand pounds on the firm's bankers, took it in cash, and decamped...'

'Rather a large amount in one hand, sir.'

Mr. Heller beat the air.

'Large amount! *You* wouldn't be so casual about it if it were your money, Cromwell. It's up to you to get it back. Dead or not dead, George Keelagher was a thief and we expect the police to deal with this as a theft. We want the money recovering and restoring...'

Mr. Craddock's voice rose to fog-horn strength again.

'You will appreciate, Cromwell, that a firm the size of Keelagher and Heller dealt in very large sums regularly.

A withdrawal of the amount mentioned would in no way put the bank on enquiry, although payable in cash to Mr. Keelagher was a bit unusual. He explained that to the bank quite glibly. He told the manager that the amount was the final sum due to him on his leaving the firm. He said he proposed to make presents to four members of his family and, to surprise them, he was giving them five thousand pounds each in cash. Knowing him to be an eccentric, the manager thought it was just another of his foibles. Keelagher didn't bank with the firm's bank, which is the Home Counties. His own account with the Northern and Southern is overdrawn several thousand pounds... That will please them, I'm sure.'

He smiled wryly.

Mr. Heller pawed the air again.

'It overdrew our own account, too, by considerably more than the security deposited...'

'It was just a casual remark by the Home Counties manager, made to Mr. Heller this morning, which lead to the discovery of this affair. We thought we'd better let you know. As far as our information goes, there was no trace of the money found when Keelagher was killed.'

'I've heard nothing about twenty thousand pounds lying about, sir. I'll telephone Superintendent Littlejohn right away, as soon as I get back to The Yard. But could you give me some more information about how you discovered that Mr. Keelagher was almost penniless? This is a very sudden development, isn't it, sir? One day he is spoken of as being very wealthy, the next he's almost a pauper.'

'When Heller rang me up about the comment of the Home Counties manager, I went round to the Northern and Southern to enquire about Keelagher's personal affairs. I'm his executor, jointly with that bank, and I felt we might look into matters together. I discovered that at one time Keelagher had a large deposit of share certificates of all kinds in safe custody at the bank, as well as substantial credit balances. Both securities and balances have been gradually whittled away, until now there's next to nothing there. As a matter of fact, the Manager of the Northern and Southern said he got the idea that Keelagher was banking elsewhere. He'd no idea which bank, but he tried tactfully to find out from Keelagher, who told him brusquely to mind his own business.'

'So, to put it briefly, it appears that Mr. Keelagher had either ruined himself by rash speculation or hidden his resources somewhere else. In the event of having ruined himself, he decided to abscond with as much money as he could gather together...'

Mr. Heller broke out again.

'There's no doubt whatever of what The Scoundrel's been up-to. He'd ruined himself with foolish speculation. As soon as the Home Counties manager made me wise about what had happened, I quickly conducted a cursory enquiry of my own. I rang up the registrars of some of the large companies in which Keelagher had investments in the old days. I was informed that he'd sold his holdings some time ago. It will be a long and difficult job of accountancy to trace and discover what he's done with the money, or how much of the firm's funds he's mishandled in addition to the impudent swindle he's performed on our banking account... But that's not all... Not by a long way... Tell him what I told you, Craddock... It makes me sick to talk about it.'

He looked it, too. He was the colour of putty and talked on and on, in a shrill voice, like a medium interpreting the conversation of spirits from another world.

'Heller tells me that when his suspicions were aroused, he opened Keelagher's private desk at the office. It was locked, but he found a key which would fit it. There was nothing whatever in the drawers. Keelagher had cleaned out the lot. But Heller made a thorough job of it by taking out the drawers and examining the cavities behind. There he found odds and ends of useless paper, including a rather obscene photograph of the kind hawked round Paris...

'The dirty old swine. I knew he had a kink of some sort, but...'

'Never mind that, Heller. Let me get this ended. Heller found a more important clue. It was an up-to-date circular about trips abroad by steamship. Luxury cruises, in a way. There was a pencil mark against a boat bound for South Africa which put in at Cannes yesterday. Now, my theory is, and Heller agrees, that Keelagher gathered together all the money he could lay his hands on and planned to disappear. He behaved as though he were taking a normal holiday with his nephew, left with them in their caravan and headed them in the direction of Cannes. Thence he planned to vanish. He would book himself a passage at the Cannes office and take the incoming boat for Africa. Nobody would have thought of that way out. They'd have assumed he'd lost himself in the wilderness where, I believe, he persuaded them to camp. I hear that it's a place where such a thing might happen. One could vanish and never be found.'

'But, surely, by going off with his nephew to the south, a trip which took a few days, he might, if the theft had been discovered, have been stopped and arrested en route...'

Mr. Heller broke in again with an angry shout which startled the other two.

'That shows The Scoundrel's cunning! He knew that the bank only sends us the statements of our banking accounts once weekly on Fridays. He awaited the receipt of the statements last Friday and at once cashed his cheque and left with his nephew for France. He'd almost a week to get away before the theft was discovered. Oh, he was crafty. He'd got it all worked out. He was going to hide somewhere pleasant and spend the rest of his days on my money. He was lucky in that somebody killed him before he caught that boat. If he'd got away, I'd have followed him to the ends of the earth. I'd have brought him to book... I'd have seen justice done... I'd have dragged him in the mud...'

Heller paused for breath.

'That will do, Heller. You're going to give yourself a stroke. Is there anything more, Cromwell? No doubt, you're as bewildered as I am about all this. Go and think it over and if we can help you in any way, call to see me again.'

Cromwell was glad to get away. He'd no wish to stimulate Heller to any further antics and possibly end up by sending for an ambulance to take him to hospital in convulsions. In spite of the care he exercised in the matter of expenses accounts, Cromwell hailed a taxi and sped off to The Yard as quickly as it would take him.

He was surprised how quickly he got through to Littlejohn. The Superintendent was back at Dorange's villa at Vence, but the police at Cannes quickly arranged for the call to be transferred there.

Cromwell reported his latest sensation.

'That throws a different light on matters altogether, old man. Now we have motive, good and proper. Somebody must have known Uncle George was carrying a heavy load of money with him and set about relieving him of it.'

'Have you found any trace of it, sir?'

'None whatever. But, it seems that, according to Waldo, Keelagher travelled with three pieces of luggage; his main suitcase, a new one; a dressing-case; and a sort of travelling chemist's shop in a smaller case full of medicines of all kinds. There were only two when we came to look around. The new suitcase wasn't there. Probably that was where the money was carried. Perhaps there was a false bottom in it.'

'What next then, sir?'

'That seems to settle my movements. I'll have to return to London on the next 'plane from Nice. The centre of gravity of the case has shifted from here back to England. I'll come over and give you a hand at your end.'

'What's happened to Waldo Keelagher and his wife?'

'They're under house arrest in an hotel in Cannes. It looks as if this will be very inconvenient for them. They're in my charge, at present. I'm responsible for them, and, without me, they'll probably be shifted to the local gaol. Which will be just too bad. I'm sorry for them. Unless, of course, Dorange will take them under his wing.'

'When will I be seeing you, then, sir?'

'I'll take the night 'plane. Don't trouble to meet me. Get some sleep and I'll be waiting for you at The Yard in the morning.'

CHAPTER NINE
THE EAVESDROPPER

It was raining when Littlejohn arrived back in England. At Nice the sun had been almost too hot to bear and the sky without a cloud. If it hadn't been for Waldo Keelagher hounding him down and getting him involved in the mystery of Great-Uncle George, he'd still have been at *Les Charmettes,* taking his ease in the shady cloisters, with the scent of roses in the air. He needn't have mixed himself in this at all. Somebody else would have handled it just as competently. But Waldo and his wife had seemed like a couple of helpless youngsters and, after all, Waldo was Cromwell's cousin...

Cromwell was at Heathrow to meet Littlejohn.

'What's it feel like to be an Inspector, old man?'

'All right. But I sometimes wish I was a sergeant again when I think of the good times we used to have together. I don't see as much of you as I used to.'

'Well, it looks as if we're going to see quite a lot of each other for a while now. Your cousin Waldo seems to have landed himself in a pretty mess through no fault of his own.'

At Scotland Yard they went to Littlejohn's room to discuss the case. The place depressed Littlejohn. The desk had been cleared, the windows closed, and the air was hot and stuffy. They opened the windows and sent for some tea. Outside, the rain was still beating down and below, the Embankment looked like a sea of umbrellas and people hurrying about to get out of the downpour.

'Yesterday, I did the rounds of the shipping offices...'

Cromwell took out his black notebook and removed the elastic band carefully, as though he expected the contents to fly out and flutter round the room.

'I thought that maybe George Keelagher had booked himself a passage either from Marseilles or Cannes in London before he left. You remember I told you about the shipping leaflet they found at the back of a drawer in his desk, with a mark against a boat bound for South Africa. He hadn't booked in his own name with any of the usual companies. Of course, he could have taken a cargo boat, perhaps from Marseilles, but that seems unlikely. So, I sent a couple of men round the travel agencies. They took Keelagher's photograph with them. They didn't have any luck, but the clerk in a small place near the Monument said Keelagher had been in a week ago and asked about flights from Nice to Corsica. And that's all.'

'Corsica? Surely he wasn't thinking of hiding-out there with his loot. I wonder where Keelagher intended to end up? Was all this chasing around just Keelagher's way of eliminating his tracks? Had he planned to hide himself somewhere and then scatter a lot of dud clues to put us off his trail? This clerk in the office near the Monument... He was sure it was Keelagher? Did he know him?'

'Yes. He was a friend of the senior clerk at Keelagher and Heller's and did most of the business for the management and staff there. He'd called to see Mr. George Keelagher a time or two in connection with holidays in the past.'

'So, George Keelagher guessed that enquiries might be made there in the event of his disappearance.'

'That's quite likely.'

'I wonder what the old boy was up to. Whatever his plans were, someone knew he was preparing to bolt with the firm's money and followed him all the way. This case is getting very complicated. If Old Keelagher was sowing clues as he travelled, how much of the information we find is going to be genuine and how much phoney and simply created by Keelagher to put us off his scent?'

'I don't know. It looks as if we'll have to start at the beginning again and work on the assumption that any clues we find might be false. In covering his tracks, Keelagher has covered his murderer as well.'

'I think I'd like to meet Miss Lucy. Will you take me there and introduce us?'

'Certainly. I was just thinking of that myself. We might ask her to unlock her brother's desk and see what we can find in it.'

The German maid opened the door to them at *Pontresina*. She wore a long face which suddenly brightened up when she saw Cromwell.

'Miss Keelagher will be glad you have come. Mr. Richley and Mrs. Benson have gone away.'

She hustled them into the presence of Miss Lucy, who didn't seem in the least perturbed by the turn of events. She was taking coffee and there was a large plate of toast on the tray in front of her.

'Good morning, Cousin Robert...'

Cromwell introduced Littlejohn.

'I'm so glad you've both called. You'll be able to help me check the contents of the house. Richley and Benson have run away and left me. I want to make sure they haven't stolen anything. You'll take coffee with me whilst we talk?'

She sent for two more cups.

'Margaret, the German maid, has been very good. *She,* at least, didn't run away at the first signs of trouble. I have sent to the agency for more servants. They should be here tomorrow. Everyone seems to be in a hurry to get away from this place nowadays. First, my brother; then Benson and Richley. I hope they don't find the bodies of Benson and Richley in some outlandish place, too. One murder in the family is quite enough.'

She didn't seem a bit put-out. Murder and embezzlement might have been everyday occurrences.

The coffee arrived, but before they settled down, Littlejohn thought something ought to be done about the vanished pair of servants.

'What made them leave, Miss Keelagher?'

'I'm sure I don't know, Superintendent. Unless, of course, Richley was a mind reader and foresaw that I was going to dismiss him as soon as I respectably could after my brother's funeral. In that case, I was sure Benson would go, too. As I told Robert, they were as thick as a couple of thieves.'

'They left hastily, I gather.'

'When Margaret got up at seven this morning, neither of them was about. She went to Benson's room and found the bed made and all Benson's belongings gone. She then went to Richley's room and found it in the same condition. They must have left early. Benson came to tell me goodnight, as usual, at ten o'clock last night. I cannot imagine they were about to run away at that hour.'

'So far, you haven't missed anything?'

'No. I don't expect it. Benson had been with me a very long time and was as honest as the day. Unless Richley had corrupted her, she wouldn't take a thing that wasn't hers. Nor, I would think, would she allow Richley to do so. Richley,

too, was *supposed* to be a man of principle, though I don't
know how far his principles extended. Benson once told
me that Richley and his brother, who lives in Fulham, were
members of some queer religious sect and, at times, officiated at revivalist services. Evangelists. Richley had an unctu-
ous way with him, you will remember, Cousin Robert...'

'In any case, we don't wish to lose touch with the pair of
them, Miss Keelagher. May I use your 'phone, please. I'd better get a message to Scotland Yard about trying to trace them.'

'Of course, Superintendent. The instrument is in the hall.'

'You'd better do it, I think, Cromwell. You've seen the
pair of them in the flesh and can give a description of them.'

Cromwell hurried about his business.

'Could I see the rooms of the two servants, Miss
Keelagher? We might find some hint as to where they've
gone?'

'Of course. I'll show you myself. Please follow me. I'm
sorry, it will be a slow procession. I'm not so active as I used
to be years ago.'

She led the way. There was an elegance and dignity
about her of times long past. The house was the same. The
stairs were broad and thickly carpeted. However much
brother and sister had disliked and ignored each other, they
had certainly attended to the comforts of life.

The house was silent, save for the kitchen at the end of a
corridor behind the stairs, where the German maid seemed
to be preparing lunch and one of Richley's machines was
whizzing and humming.

The place gave you the impression of little change over
the years. The staircase was papered in dark red with patterns
of love-lies-bleeding. The first floor, also thickly carpeted,
disclosed bedroom doors, four of them, and a bathroom
at the end of the corridor. Littlejohn suggested that he

should climb to the next floor alone, as Miss Keelagher had mounted to the first with some difficulty. But she insisted.

'I wish to see their rooms. I haven't been here for some time.'

There were four rooms there, too. Richley's was the first and Mrs. Benson's at the far end. The passage was half carpeted over oilcloth. There was an aroma of floor polish about and a queer atmosphere which seemed to arise from the architecture and fittings of the building. The windows were pointed at the top, gothic fashion, with small panes of glass. In spite of the time of year and the hot, moist August outside, it was chilly there and the long corridor with many doors, all painted brown, was forbidding, almost mysterious. The kind of place which might once have harboured the mad women, naughty children, and wicked servants of popular Victorian novelists.

Miss Keelagher must have read Littlejohn's thoughts.

'Did you ever read Henry James's *Turn of the Screw*, Superintendent?'

'Yes, Miss Keelagher.'

'Richley always reminded me of Peter Quint, the diabolical butler. In spite of his pious, pie-in-the-sky manner, I always felt that under it all, he was a thorough villain. I cannot say I wonder why my brother kept him on. My brother was a strange man himself. He never seemed to know when he was skating perilously close to danger or destruction. However, you haven't come for a description of my brother's character. Here is Richley's room.'

It was large and square and looked over the garden, which was shaded by tall old trees, the tops of which reached to the sills of the two windows. It was gloomy from lack of light through the same style of gothic windows they'd passed in the corridor. The wardrobe was a built-in affair and quite empty. The same with the dressing-table and chest of drawers. The bed had either not been slept in the night before or re-made before the occupant fled. Richley must have been a tidy man. There wasn't even a trace of paper, tobacco ash, or any of the odds and ends people leave in bedrooms. The man had gone and there wasn't a clue behind him.

There had evidently been a bell on the wall at one time, which, when removed, had left screw marks which had been painted over.

'I see there was a bell there at some time ...'

'Yes. It was a night-bell installed once when my father was here. Someone or other was gravely ill and it was there in case they needed to signal for the butler. It was later moved to the corridor outside so that one or another of the servants could hear and answer it if the butler was away.'

Littlejohn took the only chair and climbed up and examined the place on the wall. It had been tampered with fairly recently and a wire passing through it into the wall had been cut flush with it not long ago. It was still bright at the terminal. Perhaps Richley had even clipped it before he left.

'Did Richley have a wireless set in his room?'

'I never heard one. In fact, his room downstairs was fitted with both wireless and television sets. He certainly had no need for a set in this place. I'm sure there wasn't one.'

'There's a wire here which seems to have been recently cut off. I wondered ...'

Mrs. Benson's room was just the same. Neat, tidy, the bed made, the drawers and wardrobe quite empty. The removal of the pair of them had been complete. The fireplaces had been bricked up and electric radiators installed. They couldn't even burn paper or other rubbish there.

Miss Keelagher sat in the armchair beside the bed.

'I can't understand it all. As I said before, I knew Richley and Benson were hand in glove, but I'd no idea so closely. It was obviously such a close relationship, that when Richley took off, Mrs. Benson followed suit. I'm beginning to think something quite scandalous might have been going on between them under our very noses.'

Littlejohn smiled. Cromwell had given him a brief description of the two portly ageing servants of the establishment and the idea of their indulging in a strange romantic intrigue under the rafters seemed grotesque.

'He must have had a powerful hold over her somehow...'

'Or vice versa, Miss Keelagher?'

'You mean... She...?'

'Maybe.'

'I don't believe it. He was the evil one of the pair.'

Miss Keelagher was quite a woman. It was evident that she regarded Mrs. Benson as her ally and Richley as on her brother's side. Just that. And Richley was therefore the villain of the piece. Even to the extent of resembling Peter Quint.

'Does the other maid sleep on this floor?'

'No. She occupies the room next to mine. She is a German doctor's daughter here to give her services in exchange for learning English and, I presume, gather some knowledge of English life and ways...'

She'd certainly do that at *Pontresina*! True, Miss Keelagher, with her Victorian manners, her faded elegance, her eccentricities, would do her duty conscientiously to her foreign guest, but did the German doctor know about the embezzling stockbroker, the butler who resembled Peter Quint, and Mrs. Benson who somehow either held him in thrall or else was dominated by him?

'Were there ever any other servants here on this corridor with Quint... I mean Richley, and Mrs. Benson?'

'Quite a number came and went. I suppose Richley was the cause of some of them leaving, but I've forgotten most of them. I lost touch with all of them except Nellie Forty. She left to be married. She lives in Highgate now. Her husband keeps a greengrocery business.'

'Could I have her address?'

'Of course. If you've finished here, we'll go down and find it. It's in my book.'

Cromwell had done his business with Scotland Yard and was just in time to put Nellie Forty's address in his black book. 87, Tulliver Street, Highgate.

'You'll find her very helpful. She was the best maid I ever had.'

'When did she leave you?'

'About seven years ago...'

'Do you mind if I take a look around your own room, Miss Keelagher? I'm interested in what might have been at the other end of the piece of wire we found in Richley's room.'

'The bell, you mean?'

'Yes, the bell which isn't a bell any longer.'

He strolled round the room filled with heavy furniture, lined with hundreds of hard and paper-backed crime novels. There were tins of biscuits, boxes of chocolate, bottles of sweets all over the place. It was a wonder Miss Keelagher wasn't a huge mass of fat instead of a dainty bag of bones. Her sole occupations seemed to be eating and reading thrillers.

From where he was standing in the large bay window, draped in heavy velvet curtains hung on rings across a curtain-pole, he could see the full length of the chandelier, a huge bronze ring supporting a white alabaster bowl striated with brown lines like marble, attached by chains to hooks in the ceiling. Down one of the hooks a wire had been carefully passed in a cunning fashion which made it invisible from most parts of the room. Littlejohn borrowed a ladder from the kitchen and climbed it to examine the bowl. It contained a small microphone.

Richley had evidently kept himself well in touch with the affairs of the household, by listening-in to conversations in private.

'I wonder if your brother's room has been treated in the same way, Miss Keelagher.'

'What exactly are you meaning, Superintendent?'

'I think Richley installed this little thing here to find out all that was said in the room. It's a microphone. With your permission, we'll send one of our experts round and get him to verify it. He'll trace the wiring.'

'You mean that *all* I said in this room could be overheard by Richley in that way?'

'Yes.'

At first she looked as if she couldn't believe it. She asked Littlejohn the same question again and he gave her the same answer. Her face froze and the usual smile vanished, leaving a fearful grimace behind. Then she passed out. They found some brandy and gave her a drink and when she recovered, she excused herself and begged their pardon for making such a fuss.

'It came as such a shock. One doesn't like to think of being overlooked and overheard in all one does. It reminds one too much of God. The One we were taught about when we were children, who would punish us for wrongdoing. It always frightened me to death. I suppose I felt the same again when you told me.'

'May we take a look in your brother's room now, Miss Keelagher? I'm anxious to know if he, too, was a victim of Richley's curiosity.'

'Of course. Please excuse my accompanying you. It's across the hall. It's locked and here is the key. Here, too, is the key of his desk, which I told Cousin Robert I held. It's a duplicate and George didn't know of its existence. On your way, please ring for Margaret. I think I'll go to bed and have lunch served there. I don't feel very well after the shock...'

The room over the way had been similarly wired, but this time the microphone had been hidden behind a radiator, as there was no chandelier. Littlejohn wondered whether Richley's receiving-station had been fixed to cut out one or the other of the rooms, or whether, now and then, he was obliged to listen to a duet between the pair of them which they didn't know was going on.

Uncle George's room was in keeping with the rest of the place, old, stuffy and decorated in the manner of a bygone age. Heavy mahogany furniture, dark hangings, turkey red carpet, large books – the bulk of them medical, quack and orthodox – on many shelves, and a large fireplace with a huge marble surround.

The desk was as large as everything else about the room. The type once known as a secretaire, with a cupboard above the desk, which had a cylindrical roll-top beneath and then a lot of drawers below the writing-desk. The key they'd borrowed from Miss Lucy opened it easily and Littlejohn and Cromwell spent a lot of time over the contents of every part of it.

There wasn't a thing in it of any use to them in the case they were investigating. It had been thoroughly tidied-up, as though George Keelagher knew he was leaving it for ever and had removed and destroyed everything which mattered. There were books and pamphlets, circulars and old letters of no importance there, but nothing more useful than that.

There was even a secret drawer, which was empty and the backs of the drawers had no overspill, no old incriminating documents, no clues; nothing but dust. Old George had made a proper job of it before he left for good.

And with that they let themselves out of the silent house.

As Cromwell turned to fasten the front gate, he saw Miss Lucy Keelagher watching their departure round the curtains of the room on the first floor.

CHAPTER TEN
NELLIE FORTY

Number 87, Tulliver Street, Highgate, was a single-windowed shop with living accommodation above and behind it and set in the middle of a long row of other seedy shops and houses which all seemed to be struggling to withstand disintegration.

The window was packed with pyramids of second-rate fruit with a descriptive card on the end of a stick protruding from each.

Oranges – Juicy – 5 for 2/4. Lemons – Italy's Best – 6 for 2/3.
As though without the card they'd be unidentifiable.

Stale grapes hung in bunches from a rod across the window. Dusty boxes of dates and old nuts in odd corners; the relics of Christmas past. Potatoes, cabbages, carrots, turnips in boxes and baskets strewn across the front of the shop. Shelves in the shop stocked with tinned vegetables, the pictorial labels of which put to shame the so-called 'fresh' stuff. Chalked on the window itself: *Rabbits. Fresh Cod.*

Across the front of it all a sign:

JOE'S MARKET.
J. Haddock, Prop.

Littlejohn and Cromwell entered and asked right away for Mrs. Haddock.

Mr. Haddock, who sold rabbits when he could get them, was skinning one for a customer, who resembled a rabbit himself. Mr. Haddock handled his prey like a skilled dissector.

A small, stocky, moustached man, bald and grey, with sad brown eyes swimming in beery tears, as though he were mourning for the rabbit. He was twenty years older than his wife and regularly threatened to swing for her if the discrepancy in their ages ever made her betray him with another man. He eyed Littlejohn and Cromwell as though suspecting something of the kind, but, as his customer was eyeing him with similar suspicions, he controlled himself.

'She's in the room at the back and she's busy.'

They went in through a glass panelled door with privacy ensured beyond it by a red plastic curtain spread along a wire.

Nellie never worked in the shop. That had been part of her unwritten marriage contract and when Haddock got drunk and disorderly he flung it at her as a testimonial to himself.

'Wotever else I am, I never made you work in the shop...'

She was sitting at a table with a large box of monkey-nuts in front of her and a small pair of scales, weighing out nuts and putting them in little transparent paper-bags. Sixpence a time.

The place was clean, furnished cheaply, and had a large grimy window at the end remote from the shop, which over-looked a yard littered with old baskets, boxes and crates and backed by another parallel row of squalid old property. There was a smell of over-ripe oranges, cabbages and fish over all.

Nellie Haddock, née Forty, was a pleasant, dark, buxom little woman, going on for fifty, with a smile and a bright, humorous eye and red cheeks in spite of her present unhealthy environment. You wondered at the source of her apparent happiness. Perhaps in spite of her husband's threats, she had a lover – certainly not the melancholy Haddock – and one day, Mr. Haddock would come upon them in this dim, almost underground retreat, do them both in, and deftly dissect them as he did his rabbits and cod, and then fulfil his promise and swing.

That was what Littlejohn felt about it as he scented an atmosphere of incompatibility and repression about the place and the smiling figure rose to meet them in the half light.

Nellie Haddock seemed happier than ever when they mentioned *Pontresina*.

'How's Miss Lucy? I saw in the paper about Mr. George. The poor old man.'

She paused and shed a ready tear, blew her nose, and smiled again.

'Not that I'd much to like him for. The old basket! The way he treated Miss Lucy. Bullying her and sending her sarcastical notes because they weren't on speaking terms. And me, too. He treated me awful. Do you know, when he'd been out on a spree and came home with one over the eight, he'd put a match to all the fires I'd laid ready for mornin' ...'

Littlejohn gave her brief news about Miss Keelagher and Nellie said she was relieved that she hadn't took it bad.

'How long were you with them, Mrs. Haddock?'

'Nearly twenty years, sir. I was there when Miss Lucy's father died. Proper nice old gent he was. Paralysed when he died. Miss Lucy and me had to do everything for him. I was only about... Let me see ...'

She gave them statistics. She'd started at *Pontresina* when she was seventeen. She'd been there twenty years and had been married to Joe Haddock for seven. She then looked baffled, as her age was forty-six. Two years had somehow got lost...

'Was Mrs. Benson there then?'

'She came after I started there. Miss Lucy couldn't manage with just me and a daily. Then Mr. George came and took-up there. Without so much as a by-your-leave, he came.'

'Bringing Mr. Richley with him?'

Nellie looked angry and then cautiously cast her eyes in the direction of the door with the red curtain, as though if Haddock overheard what she was about to say, he would *do* Richley right away.

'He was always a swine, that Richley. If it hadn't been for 'im, I might have been there yet instead of marryin' Haddock and bein' here.'

She cast a contemptuous look around her and thumped the pile of monkey nuts as though they were the cause of it all.

In the shop, people kept coming and going, preventing the jealous Haddock from intruding to investigate.

'How long did you stay at *Pontresina* after Richley arrived?'

'Nearly a dozen years, at a guess. I didn't like him from the start. He was too fresh and free. When Mrs. Benson introduced me to 'im, as Miss Nellie Forty, "Forty what?" he says. And there were other things, too.'

She looked at the two men as though wondering if they weren't old enough to learn the awful truth.

'Such as...?'

'Well, his room was next to mine and he used to pray out loud before he got in bed. I could hear the bed creak after

he'd said Amen. It was a long time before he tried to get fresh
with me. Then, one day, he said he used to pray for me. I told
'im he needn't bother, and locked my door every night after
that. He tried to persuade me to go with him to a meeting-
house where he preached sometimes on Sunday nights.'

'You went?'

'I did not. I was scared stiff. Then, he suggested we had
a word of prayer together in his room before we slept. After
that, I knew that either him or me would have to go. I put a
chair under the knob of my bedroom door and next day I
gave my notice. Haddock had been pressin' me to become
the second Mrs. H. and I thought even that better than
Richley and his prayers and his Sunday night love-feasts, as
he called his mission-hall meetin's.'

'What were the relations between Richley and Mrs.
Benson?'

'Relations? Oh, she was another he prayed for. Soon
they was prayin' together. I won't say any more. It was
disgustin'. She ought to 'ave known better. She was glad
when I gave my notice, I know. She didn't trust Richley.
And yet, she seemed fascinated by him. He could do anythin' with her.'

'They've both just left Miss Lucy's together. Perhaps
they've gone off to get married.'

'Married! Don't make me laugh. Richley wasn't the marryin' sort.'

'Where would they go if they left Miss Lucy's? Had either
of them a home?'

'Richley used to go to his brother's in Fulham all his free
time. His brother was the religious sort, too. I met him once.
They might have been twins, only Richley was bald and his
brother well covered. I think Richley had been tellin' his

brother about me. I'm sure Joel came to *Pontresina* to look me over. It was just like them. A real pair of 'oly weazels.'

'What was Richley's Christian name?'

'Eli. But in service it wasn't considered a very suitable one. So, he was always known as William.'

'Mrs. Benson. Had she any relative?'

'Not when I left. But she once had a sister who'd left her a little terrace house in Shepherd's Bush. She'd kept it on and she went there when she'd any time off or took a holiday. She used to say she always liked to feel she'd a place to go to and lay her head if the worst came to the worst.'

'Shepherd's Bush?'

'Yes. But that was seven years since. I haven't seen any of them since. I wanted to keep out of Richley's way. He was up to no good. Miss Lucy and me has written always at Christmas.'

Seven years was a long time and Nellie Haddock wasn't likely to have anything useful to tell them relating to the murder of George Keelagher.

'Was Miss Lucy good-looking in those days?'

'Oh, yes. She was rather a beauty, but her father living with her and being so ill and wantin' her day and night, it tied her for the best years of her life. By the time he died, she'd grown old beyond her years. She'd have had enough chances, plenty of them, if she'd been able to take them.'

'Was there a man called Herbert keen on her during your time there?'

'Herbert? 'erbert... I seem to remember that name. Why, yes. Of course. He worked in Mr. George's office. He called a time or two on business. One day, I remember it well, Mr. George was ill with a gastric stomach and he telephoned for some medicine that Herbert was to bring from a

London chemist's. Mr. George wouldn't ever have a doctor. He always doctored himself...'

'So Herbert came to *Pontresina?*'

It sounded very romantic!

'That's right.'

'And ...'

'He met Miss Lucy on his way out. She was goin' out for a breath of fresh air in the park. They walked down the road together. I don't remember what Herbert even looked like after all this time. All I know is that he was smaller than Miss Lucy and I thought what a poor pair they'd look at the altar, with her taller than him. But they must have fallen for one another. Next thing, she started to go out early in the evenin's all dressed up. She never told anybody where she was goin', but I'm sure she was meetin' Herbert in the park.'

'How did it all end?'

'Mark my words, Richley got to know and told Mr. George. Because, soon after, it all stopped. I don't know how. But Miss Lucy seemed to grow older and hard after that and sort of went inside herself.'

'What was Herbert's surname?'

'I've forgotten it. It's so long since. It was a queer name. Wait. I had a little joke of my own about him. Richley was all for Heaven, or so he said. Herbert's name was somethin' to do with Hell.'

'Heller?'

'That's it! Heller. Do you know him?'

'No. But my friend here does. He's now Mr. George's partner.'

'He's got on, hasn't he? Perhaps Mr. George bought him out from Miss Lucy, in a manner of speakin' ..."

Littlejohn took out an old envelope and drew on it a rough picture of the silver box they'd found containing arsenic in George's pocket. The French police had retained it as an exhibit.

'Did you ever see a little silver box like that when you were in Miss Lucy's employ, Mrs. Haddock?'

She looked hard at the drawing and then, taking it to the window, she scrutinised it carefully again.

'It looks like Miss Lucy's saccharine box. She always took care of her figure and was sparing in sugar in those days. She used to carry it in a bottle in her bag, but later got that little box for her tablets. I'm sure that's it. And I'm sure Herbert... Mr. Hell... gave it to her, because she started to use it just after they'd met. It must have been his only present to her. Why? Is it missin'?'

'No. It's still in use.'

At this, the door and the curtain were suddenly moved and Mr. Haddock stood in the doorway, wiping fish from his hands on a damp rag. A gust of fishy air followed him in.

'Wot's goin' on 'ere? It's time you'd finished them nuts, Nellie. We 'aven't all day.'

He looked Littlejohn and Cromwell up and down as though measuring his strength against the pair of them.

Mrs. Haddock introduced them.

'Police! What the 'ell?"

Littlejohn explained the reason for their visit.

'She won't be much use to yer on that account. It's seven years since she was with the Keelaghers and she hasn't seen any of them since. That's right, isn't it, Nellie?'

He seemed to challenge her to say it wasn't.

'That's right.'

'A good thing for you it was. Them Keelaghers ought to 'ave been cut down to size years since. Snobs. That's what they were. Snobs. George Keelagher's ended up like all snobs ought to end. Done in. To 'ell with 'im.'

'Joe!!'

'Don't you Joe me. They're all a lot of no-goods, growin' rich at the expense of workers like me.'

Once, in his courting days, when Joe Haddock had been afire for Nellie, delivered the greengroceries at the side door of *Pontresina* for the boss he then worked for, and was at the same time pursuing Nellie with his importunities, Richley had set the dog on him. Joe had never forgotten it. In fact, he'd been a militant communist ever since, eager to bring all the snobs low.

'She ought to thank me on 'er bended knees for takin' her away from the likes of them. A slavey, that's wot she was. If I'd my way…'

He thumped the table, as though it, too, were a snob, and tipped over the box of nuts.

There were monkey nuts all over the place and Littlejohn and Cromwell left Joe on all fours picking them up whilst Nellie held her sides and wept with laughter.

'Blowed if you don't look like a monkey yourself, Joe Haddock,' she was saying. 'You and your nuts.'

Chapter Eleven
Shepherd's Bush

Miss Annie Benson's name was on the roll of electors for all the Shepherd's Bush district to see. Cromwell, who looked it up, was surprised; not at the fact of her inclusion there, but at the lack of difficulty in obtaining a straight and easy answer to a police enquiry. He and Littlejohn made their way to 42, Metropolitan Terrace, so called in honour of the appearance of the Underground at the time when the street was opened. It was composed of several blocks of small neat terraced houses, with little tidy gardens in front. In one of the gardens they came upon Mr. William (né Eli) Richley smoking a curved pipe and gathering a bunch of flowers.

'He seems to have hung up his hat already,' remarked Cromwell.

When he saw Cromwell, the idyllic expression on Richley's face faded out and his pipe fell among the stocks and asters.

'Wot are you doing here?'

'I might ask you the same, Mr. Richley. This is Superintendent Littlejohn. Do you mind if we come inside?'

Richley hesitated, hunted for his pipe among the vegetation, found it, wiped it on his waistcoat and made a poor show of lighting it. He looked a model of indolent domesticity. He wore carpet slippers and was in his shirt sleeves. Before the intrusion of the police he had seemed settled and content. Now, he raised his hands – one still holding his bunch of flowers – as though fighting off his ill luck.

'What do you want to disturb us for? Followin' people about the country as though they was criminals. It's h'intolerable. Haven't we had enough?'

'We've a few questions we'd like you to answer. You and Mrs. Benson, who lives here, I presume ...'

'Mrs. Richley, if you please. We were married yesterday.'

'Congratulations!'

Cromwell almost made a crack about a wife giving evidence against her husband, but refrained at the last minute. It hardly seemed fair in the circumstances.

'Thank you. I hope your sentiments are authentic and not sarcastic. You can come in if you wish. In fact, you'd better. I don't want all the street talking about the police callin' and us only just taken up residence here.'

'Nice garden you've got.'

'Good of you to say so. My own work. Always fond of a bit o' garden, and whilst I was with the Keelaghers, Mrs. Benson used to allow me to look after this bit for her. One is nearer God's 'eart in a garden ...'

He couldn't help lapsing into his evangelical Fulham speech now and then, but this was an abuse of the habit and Mr. Richley paused, coughed behind his hand, and looked elsewhere.

'So now you're able to give the garden day and night service, so to speak.'

Richley gave Cromwell a dirty reproachful look.

'You'd better come inside, both of you. I'd have thought you'd something better to do than indulge in humour on a man's honest efforts.'

He led the way indoors, like one who owned the house already. It was as neat inside as out. A real, tidy spinster's retreat, with a bamboo hatstand in the hall and a picture of Lake Lucerne – probably as Mrs. Benson's father had known it – beside it. A modest carpet on the narrow stairs and a home-made woollen rug in the lobby. Mrs. Benson had never been married until Richley led her to the altar, or wherever he led her. The *Mrs.* was the kind of honorary degree assumed by certain ladies who hold senior posts in domestic service.

Mrs. Benson, now Mrs. Richley, was in the front room waiting for the worst. She'd seen Cromwell leaning over the garden fence and knew there was something amiss. Cromwell first congratulated her on her new state, then introduced Littlejohn. She was too overcome to say anything, but stood horrified on the home-made hearthrug. There was an enlarged photograph of her father in a frame over the mantelpiece, and an old piano in one corner. The rest of the furniture consisted of old-fashioned but solid chairs and tables. There was a book of hymn-tunes on the music-stand of the piano. It was open at 'Nearer my God to Thee', which reminded Cromwell of Smith, the Brides in the Bath man, and he imagined Richley singing and playing before committing something as bad as Smith did.

Richley thought it becoming to be tenderly aggressive in the presence of his new bride.

'These gentlemen have called to ask a few questions, Annie dear. I will deal with them alone and dispose of them quickly. Then you won't be upset. Wait for us in the kitchen, love.'

And he solicitously piloted her by the elbow to the door, tenderly cast her out, and closed it again.

'I won't 'ave her upset. Now, if you'll be so good as to be brief.'

He was still holding the bunch of flowers, gazed blankly at them as though he wondered where they came from, and then thrust them in a jug with a picture of Mr. Pecksniff – who resembled Richley – on it, standing on top of the piano beside a portrait of Mrs Benson and the sister who had left her the house in her will.

'You'd better sit down. We're overlooked from across the street and there's no point in giving food for gossip. We'd better *look* friendly at least.'

So they all sat down like the members of a committee.

'Now,' said Mr. Richley again.

Littlejohn left it to Cromwell.

'You left *Pontresina* in a hurry. Why?'

Mr. Richley looked hurt.

'What was there to remain there for? Miss Lucy was preparing to discharge me or ask for my resignation and Mrs. Benson, as she then was, had sworn not to remain there if I left. We had been good friends for many years and the present seemed an appropriate time for us to be married. We'd intended doing so at a convenient occasion.'

Richley rolled out the long words, almost frothing at the mouth as he vocally underlined them.

'But to pack-up and leave in the night... It seems a queer way of terminating your services, doesn't it? Most inconvenient for Miss Lucy, I'd say, especially at a time when she is bereaved.'

'She never considered our convenience. And, as for being bereaved, she didn't behave as if she was. One might almost venture to say that she was pleased about her brother's decease. She was an eccentric and exacting old woman and we were both sure there would be 'arsh words and vituperations when we gave notice and told her we wished to leave right away.'

Cromwell thrust his hands in his trousers' pockets and sat back comfortably. Outside, a man halted at the house, knocked, and told Mrs. Richley, who answered the door, that he'd called to read the gas meter. They could hear him shambling down the cellar steps. All conversation ceased until he'd done his job, which didn't take long.

'Let's begin at the beginning, Mr. Richley. When did Miss Lucy hint to you that she was going to dispense with your services?

'She didn't say it in so many words. She just showed it in her behaviour and in certain insinuations. That was enough for me.'

'Perhaps you overheard her telling me or someone else over the microphone you'd installed in her room.'

All Richley's high colouring vanished, leaving the bilious yellow undertone.

'I don't know what you're talkin' about.'

But he did.

'We know all about it. We found the remains of your apparatus. You only removed one end of it in your hurry. How long have the two rooms been wired, and why?'

They could almost hear Richley's mind working at top speed to find an appropriate excuse. It was not long in coming. His face cleared with relief.

'I have always been mechanically minded. I thought it would be a good idea, when I had been at *Pontresina* a little time, to install microphones in the respective rooms of Miss Lucy and Mr. George. It enabled me to anticipate their requirements. They were both getting on in years and it...well, it kept me in touch with them in case of need.'

'I'm sure it did. And, I would think, gave you quite a lot of information to which you weren't entitled, too. However, we'll pass the ethics of it. We're too busy to press you for all the gossip and the rest that went on during the time you were listening-in to your employers...'

Richley flushed and began to splutter.

'I must protest. It was done with nothing but good intentions...'

'I said we'd pass that. We're now concerned with a murder case. The murder of your late employer. What do you know about that and what did you hear which might have given rise to it?'

Richley turned a speechless grey. Cromwell waited for him to recover.

'You're not suggesting that I had anything to do with the murder of Mr. Keelagher, are you? Because if you are...'

'I'm suggesting nothing. I want to know anything you picked-up on your eavedropping machine which might have any bearing on the case.'

'There was nothing, I do assure you. I'm willing to co-operate to help you bring to justice the evil wretch who caused Mr. Keelagher's death, but I can think of nothing...'

Which was probably true. Richley could think of nothing but how to save himself from the mess he was in.

'Did Mr. Keelagher have any visitors just before he left for the Continent?'

'Do you mean long before, or let us say, in the same week?'

'I said *just before*. Did he?'

'Nobody except Mr. Heller, unless anyone called whilst I was absent.'

'What did Mr. Heller call for? You probably tuned-in to their talk, didn't you?'

'I ... ahem ...'

'You'd better tell us without any more hemming and hawing. If you don't tell us quietly here, we shall have to ask you to accompany us to Scotland Yard.'

Littlejohn smiled. Cromwell, as though fascinated by Richley's high falutin' manner of speech, was falling into a pompous manner himself.

'Don't do that. It would greatly h'upset Mrs. Richley.'

'It probably would. Well?'

'They discussed each time the partnership in the business.'

'What was said?'

'They were quarrelling ... High words, much of the time. It seemed Mr. Keelagher wished Mr. Heller to pay him out more substantially than Mr. Heller wished.'

'Well?'

'Well what?'

'You don't mean to tell me that having gathered what the conversation was about, you politely swiched-off and went away. Not an inquisitive man like you, Mr. Richley, surely.'

'I resent...'

'*What did they say!* Did they have a violent quarrel?'

Richley mopped his sweating head.

'Very embarrassing. You see, it concerned Miss Lucy, too. I hope you'll keep this confidential. It seems Mr. Heller and Miss Lucy were at one time, ahem ... well ... Mr. Heller was paying attentions to Miss Lucy. It was a long time ago, I imagine. It came out in the course of angry words, that Mr. Keelagher had given Mr. Heller a small partnership in the firm in consideration of his ceasing to ahem ..."

'Ceasing to woo his sister?'

'I *beg* your pardon Yes, yes, yes. As you say. Mr. Heller accepted the proposition, it seems. My opinion of Mr. Heller suffered when I heard that, I can assure you.'

'Did it, indeed? I wonder what Mr. Heller's opinion would have been of you, listening-in to all that was said. Go on ...'

'Go on? What am I to tell you?'

'What *you* overheard.'

'It was mostly abuse, high words, vituperation. But to summarise what it was all about...'

Richley leaned towards Cromwell, who in turn leaned back to avoid the spray which Richley cast-up in his enthusiasm.

'To put it brief, Mr. Keelagher h'expressed his intention of ending completely his share in the partnership and retiring. He said he had remained half a partner long enough and had only done that to extract from Mr. Heller the full sum due to him. A further twenty thousand pounds, he said. Mr. Heller, if I may use such a metaphor, raised the roof. The loud way he shouted caused the microphone to rattle. He said he would never agree. That he hadn't such a sum available. Not half of it. Mr. Keelagher thereupon told him to borrow it from the bank against the securities that Mr. Heller had already deposited there. They quarrelled for a long time.'

A pause. Richley mopped himself again.

'May I have a drink, please?'

'Of course.'

Richley made for the door, listening at the panel before he opened it, as though this were his professional habit which he couldn't break, even in his own home. When he opened it, Mrs. Richley was standing listening on the other side. Richley was surprised.

'Is anything the matter, my dear?'

'I was just coming to see if you were all right.'

Richley's life must have been eternally complicated by eavesdropping in one way or another!

'Everything is all right, but I do not wish you to join us. It would upset you. We are discussing the murder.'

He went to refresh himself and returned smelling strongly of sherry. It must have been of the cooking variety, for it made him hiccup and clutch his breastbone as it hit his stomach.

'You were telling us about the security at the bank.'

'Ah, yes. Pray excuse me ...'

Richley writhed and heaved, as though dislodging the sherry from somewhere inside him.

'Mr. Keelagher then said Mr. Heller could take the money from the firm's account at the bank against the securities which Mr. Heller had placed there. There was more argument and then Mr. Keelagher told Mr. Heller he'd better agree or it would be the worse for him. Mr. Heller then said, "Are you trying to blackmail me?", and Mr. Keelagher laughed and said "Exactly. Twenty thousand, or you go to gaol."'

Richley whispered it as though villainy were quite alien to him and horrified him. Then he hiccupped violently.

'Beg pardon. Mr. Heller left shortly after that. Although he said nothing much afterwards, I gather he agreed to Mr. Keelagher's suggestion.'

'Anything else?'

'Not on that occasion.'

'I've guessed that. But have you overheard anything which might throw light on the murder?'

'Oh dear, no. I'm afraid I can't assist you there. I haven't the faintest idea who did the dastardly thing.'

'Did you overhear anything which revealed where Mr. Keelagher proposed to go when he retired?'

'Not exactly. I overheard him telephoning a time or two to Mr. Waldo about the trip to the South of France. I know that, at first, Mr. Waldo and his wife were going to another place ... Bordeaux, I think it was. I know it was a wine district.

Thence, they proposed to go to the Mediterranean. But Mr. George made them change their plans on account of his wishing to study the ways of certain insects which, I believe, have a habit of prayer...'

Littlejohn smiled. The prayer, in a manner of speaking, was grace before meat with the praying mantis!

'He wished to change the route to get more quickly to the place where the insects lived. Mr. Waldo was disappointed, but finally agreed.'

'Did you come upon an idea of where Mr. Keelagher was going from there?'

'I did overhear him telephoning one morning when he stayed at home clearing up his affairs before the holidays. And he *did* clear them up. Thoroughly. He must have intended never to return.'

Richley turned pale again.

'He may have known the fate which awaited him!'

'The telephone?'

'Ah, yes. He was apparently speaking to some tourist or shipping company. He was asking about a trip to Canada. He had relatives there and I know they'd invited him to go and see them. That must have been in his mind.'

'Tell me what was said about the trip.'

'I gathered roughly that he wished to know how to get to Canada from...what was the place...?'

'Cannes?'

'No...Nice, that was it. Nice. My former employers went there frequently...'

'Could you hear both ends of this conversation?'

'Of course not. But Mr. Keelagher must have been taking it down and talking to himself as he did so. The suggestion was that he should fly to New York by the American 'plane from Nice and go thence to Canada. Mr. Keelagher seemed to agree. He seemed surprised that he would need a special permit to enter America...'

'A visa?'

'That was the word, I recollect. A veeesah!'

He said it like a fish gobbling down ant-eggs.

'He seemed taken with the idea. That, I think, is all I can tell you.'

'But you had Miss Lucy's room wired, too. What about her conversations? Did he tell her good-bye?'

'No. They never spoke. Just communicated by notes. They had quarrelled.'

'About Heller. Was he ever mentioned?'

'She used to talk to my wife about a certain Herbert. I gather that was Mr. Heller. There had been a love affair, but it ended through Mr. George's intervention.'

'Returning to Miss Lucy's room, which was wired, did you ever overhear anything going on there which might give us an idea about the murder?'

'I can't think of anything, sir. You see, Miss Lucy rarely went out or received visitors. The only person she engaged much in conversation was my wife, Mrs. Benson, as she then was. In the normal conversation of good friends, Mrs. Benson and I used to exchange news and she told me anything of importance in Miss Lucy's day. I used the microphone very little.'

'On the rare occasions that you did use it, what then?'

Richley had grown anxious and pop-eyed. He was obviously holding something back. Cromwell returned to the attack.

'Shall I tell you something, Mr. Richley? I believe you and your wife ran away from *Pontresina* because you were afraid of what is happening now. A police enquiry, and your being questioned. You knew things had been going on there. You knew too much for your own comfort, in fact. So, as matters warmed up, you beat a retreat. Why you retreated here, I can't imagine. You might have known we'd come to this place almost the first. What are you hiding?'

Richley tried to recover his shattered dignity.

'I must tell you, as you don't seem h'aware of it, I have a conscience. I have my principles. For many years, Mrs. Richley and I have been in the employ of the Keelagher family and lived under their roof. We had no desire to be forced by the police to disclose information which we regarded as sacrosanct...'

He put his face close to Cromwell's and spat it at him. Cromwell frowned and used his handkerchief vigorously.

'Go on, but you've no need to shout. This sacrosanct information... the inviolable secret which you fled rather than disclose. What is it? You'd better tell us. Remember, your devotion to the family calls for co-operation with the police to find who killed Mr. George.'

Littlejohn rose to stretch his legs and looked through the window. Cromwell was using the right, word-bandying technique with Richley, but it was a bit of a bore. Outside the sun was shining on the typical London suburban street. There was even a man hawking muffins and the chimney of one of the cottages was on fire and pouring out clouds of black smoke. A bobby was knocking at the door...

'Well, I suppose I'd better tell you, although it's not a thing I like to do. Miss Lucy saw Mr. Heller shortly before Mr. George left.'

'Did she, by gad, and you kept this up your sleeve all this time. Go on.'

'It seems she had refused ever to see him again. According to Mrs. Richley, who was always in Miss Lucy's confidence, Heller has written to her a time or two of late, but Miss Lucy had thrown his letter on the fire unread. Mrs. Richley finally persuaded her to read the last one that came. She pointed out, it might contain something important.'

'Very convincing. Go on.'

'Miss Lucy read it. She seemed surprised. She didn't confide in my wife what it was about, but telephoned Mr. Heller and made an arrangement to see him, when, of course, Mr. George was not at home.'

'You, I gather, listened to the telephone conversation.'

Mr. Richley was on his dignity.

'I admit I did. I was apprehensive about Miss Lucy. She had nobody to look after her. I wished to know if I could help in any way.'

'Why didn't you ask her?'

'Being, what, in a manner of speaking one would call Mr. George's man, I suffered somewhat from the same treatment she meted out to Mr. George. She was very distant and reticent with me.'

Cromwell sympathised with her!

'And what was the end of it all?'

'Mr. Heller came to see her.'

'And you, of course, officiated at the other end of the eavesdropper?'

'I do resent your sarcasm. I'm only trying to help. Why keep being so rude to me?'

'Go on.'

'The interview did not last long. Miss Lucy was very much aloof. Mr. Heller said he felt she ought to know that her brother was, in Mr. Heller's view, planning to leave the country for good. Miss Lucy, much to my surprise and, I gather, to Mr. Heller's, said she was well aware of it. Mr. Heller stated that Mr. George had cleaned up all his affairs at the office and Mr. Heller, who had been keeping an eye on his behaviour, had discovered Mr. George had been realising securities for cash, as though proposing to take all his resources with him.'

Miss Lucy, who was in the habit of rifling George's desk, must have been pursuing a similar line of enquiry.

'What next?'

'Mr. Heller then said that, although he had greatly wronged Miss Lucy in the past, he had never ceased to have a high regard for her. He had never married...At this, Miss Lucy cut him short and told him she didn't wish to hear more about it. Had he finished? Mr. Heller then went on to say the real purpose of his visit was to warn Miss Lucy that she'd better be sure the family trust was safe, as her very livelihood depended on her income from it. He feared that Mr. George might abuse the trust and run away with the funds, too. She coldly replied that she was well aware of that, too, and had already assured herself that the funds were h'intact. Miss Lucy, sir, was, to put it in the vernacular, a corker. A corker, sir.'

'I think you're right there, Mr. Richley. Was that all? Did the interview end there?'

Richley began to look uneasy again. He'd hoped to evade more awkward details, but Cromwell hung on.

'Mr. Heller then seemed to lose his temper. He seemed to get angry because Miss Lucy treated him so coldly. He'd perhaps expected her to, so to speak, join forces with him to prevent Mr. George going. Instead, she'd told him she knew it all and was apparently doing nothing about it. Mr. Heller commented on this. He told her that if *she* was unmoved by Mr. George absconding with the money, *he* wasn't. He said Mr. George had ruined his life and happiness and he wasn't going to allow him to do anything more to him. Rather than tolerate it longer he'd...'

'Yes?'

'He was only speaking in a rage, Inspector. I do beg of you not to place too serious a complexion on it. I've no wish to make statements which might 'ang an innocent person. Mr. Heller said rather than put up with any more of the hell on earth, he'd rather kill Mr. George. Miss Lucy, thereupon, rang for my wife and told her Mr. Heller was leaving. That was all.'

'It ended there, then?'

'Except that on the way out, Mr. Heller apologised for his outburst. They stood talking in whispers in the hall for at least ten minutes and Miss Lucy, my wife said, seemed very upset afterwards.'

'I suppose, this whispered conversation was held outside the range of your ear-aid and you didn't gather what it was about?'

'I didn't hear it.'

Richley said it pompously as though there were some virtue in it.

'That was all?'

'H'absolutely all.'

'Very good. And now, would you kindly, just as a matter of routine, tell me where you and Mrs. Benson, now Mrs. Richley, were on the day Mr. George met his death?'

Richley stood up and recoiled a step as he did so.

'You don't mean to tell me, that after all I've told you, after I've collaborated and co-operated with you, you suspect my wife and me of murdering Mr. George! It's preposterous. How could we?'

'I said it's mere routine. Tell me, and that part of the matter will end if your replies are satisfactory.'

'They are. H'eminently so. We were at *Pontresima* all the time. All the time. Miss Lucy will confirm that. Also

Margaret. Also, if you wish it my wife and I will confirm that both of us were there all the time.'

Cromwell noted it in his black notebook, the very sight of which seemed to give Richley quite a turn.

'What about Miss Lucy herself? Where was she?'

'At *Pontresina,* of course. Where else? She was never one for going far afield. Always in her room, reading blood-and-thunders. My wife and I, as well as the German maid, can confirm that.'

'I think we'd better have Mrs. Richley in now.'

'I hope you're not going to put her through the ordeal I've been put through this afternoon. I shall protest... complain to the authorities. I...'

'Just a word. That's all.'

Mr. Richley went to the door, listened at the panel as was his professional habit, then opened it. His wife was, also professionally on the mat listening-in. He seemed surprised again.

'I was just coming in to ask if you'd all like a cup of tea.'

'Not just now, my dear. The gentlemen are going. Would you come inside?'

He led her carefully in.

'The Inspector wishes to ask you to confirm that Miss Lucy was indoors all the day that Mr. George passed away.'

Mrs. Richley, starved of words by being cast out from the conference, prepared herself for a deluge.

'That poor lady never stirs out much. She always...'

'Excuse me. I don't want to disturb you by taking up more of your time. Was Miss Lucy at home the day before and on the actual day that Mr. George died?'

'She was. She wasn't very well and stayed in bed all day. That was the day before. I can vouch for that. She didn't get up till noon the day her brother passed-on.'

She seemed, probably though long association with him, to have contracted some of her husband's unction. He stood there, regarding her with pride.

'You, Mrs. Richley, and the German maid were also indoors all the time?'

'Of course. I went out shopping for an hour in the afternoon before Mr. George passed on. Nothing else. Margaret, the maid, didn't go out at all. As for my husband, he was indoors all the time.'

Cromwell made a note of it. He didn't much care for 'passing-on' in the case of Uncle George. George had been murdered. Somebody had passed him on. He put that in his book by way of a little joke.

'That will be all for the present. I thank you both. I hope you'll be remaining here for a while, till we've sorted matters out.'

'Of course. We propose to retire now. We don't wish to enter into service again, Mr. Cromwell. My wife agrees with me, I know.'

'Very well. By the way, Mrs. Ben...Richley. I believe Mr. George had relations in Canada. A monk or a priest? Do you know exactly where he lives?'

Richley intervened.

'I could tell you, I think...Mr. George used to write to him now and then and he called once when he was in England. He and Mr. George got on very well. I think he was Mr. George's best friend of the family. I remember the good man's address from the letters I used to post. I have a good memory.'

He closed his eyes modestly and smiled.

'Let me see. Brother Martin, Abbey of the Holy Trinity, Montreal, Canada. Quite easy to remember.'

'Thank you very much...'

Richley saw them to the door, having again conducted his wife to the rear quarters of the house, like a gaoler replacing an inmate in a cell. As they left, he gave them a slight professional bow and closed the door softly as though shutting in his secrets again.

Chapter Twelve
Fraud Squad

A Long-Distance call to Montreal from Scotland Yard brought Father Martin to the telephone. The priest was actually a quiet man, but the experience of trans-ocean telephoning and a certain nervousness made him sound loud, large and exuberant. He was thunderstruck to hear of the violent death of George Keelagher.

'He was due to join me here early next month.'

Littlejohn, at the other end of the line, allowed him to recover his balance and then began to question him.

'Did he intend to stay for good, Father?'

'That all depended on circumstances. Last time I was over visiting him, I found he had lost much of his bitterness and enthusiasm for business life. He said he envied me and the quiet life I was leading. I told him the same life could be his if he wished it and was prepared to make certain sacrifices. We met several times and before I left, he said he would think over the matter of coming to live here, in the monastery.'

That was a surprise for Littlejohn! Uncle George, whom almost everybody hated, Uncle George, the absconder, about to become a monk!

'Not that. He felt he had no calling to join the order. He wished to live in the side we reserve for guests and a number of lay brothers. He said he was sick of the rush of life and wanted peace in which to pursue his studies. He was a naturalist, you know.'

It almost seemed appropriate; to study the praying mantis in a monastery!

'So, you expected to see him soon?'

'We arranged to meet in New York on the 4th of next month. Thence, after he had spent a few days in the Library of Natural History there, we proposed to return to Montreal. There, after consideration, George would decide whether to stay on or not. I am very grieved at what has happened. I'm sure he would have found happiness here with us.'

So that was why George Keelagher had gathered up his money and belongings, and apparently someone else's as well, and tried to make his roundabout way to a 'plane for America.

And yet, he could not have hoped to get away with it. He must have known that sooner or later, even if only through passport and visa records, the police would find him. All the same, retreat to a monastery was a good idea. Nobody would think of hunting for a man like George Keelagher in such a place.

When he had finished with the good Father Martin, Littlejohn made his way to the office of Superintendent Flight of the Fraud Squad.

Flight was a man who could not abide hot weather. It seemed to paralyse him. He was sitting in his dusty room poring over ledgers and wearing only his shirt and trousers. He was even minus his braces and shoes. Although everybody knew about his peculiarity, he always made a point of politely apologising for it.

'Glad to see you, Littlejohn. This hot weather! I wish to God it would rain or snow. It's killing me. Excuse the dishabille. I'd work stark naked if it were decent to do so. I can't get cool.'

He passed his hand over the piles of books and papers on his desk.

'Here's the cashier of a bucket-shop which calls itself a bank, vanished into the blue after cooking the books to the tune of twenty-five thousand pounds. Why do they have to find it out in the middle of a sweltering August? Why can't they wait till a cold, foggy day in November...? What can I do for you, Littlejohn?'

Flight, tall, elderly, an ex-Inspector of Taxes, who had joined the police for a bit of peace, was one of the smartest men in the country on fraudulent book-keeping and figuring. His long, pale, sad face, topped by thin grey hair and a monkish tonsure, belied his intelligence. For some professionals to know that Flight was mixed in their affairs was almost enough to make them give themselves up without a struggle.

'I've a bit of a problem here I'd like your advice about. The funny thing is, I've not got it clear in my mind. I can't even put it to you ship-shape.'

'Let's go to *The Bunch of Grapes* and sort it out over some cold beer.'

Flight began to dress himself. Soon he was ready, looking like a dapper elderly broker going to the City to do some broking, whatever that might be. His ragged moustache had even assumed a military brightness. They descended to the underground *Bunch* in one of the maze of streets off the Embankment.

'That's better,' said Flight, as he ordered two more. 'Now to business.'

Littlejohn told Flight all about George Keelagher. Flight smiled grimly at the name Uncle George. His own name was Horace, but in family circles, he, too, was known as Uncle George. It seemed like setting one George to catch another. As Littlejohn told his tale, Flight scribbled notes on the back of a card advertising beer which he'd taken from the wall.

George Keelagher, Stockbroker.

Family Trust. Private Investment Trust.

Dissolution of Partnership.

Withdrawal of £20,000 from Bank.

Bank overdraft secured by George Keelagher and Herbert Heller, partners in the firm.

Keelagher Blackmailing Heller?

That was all.

Flight drank the last of his beer and ordered another.

'When we've finished this, we'll go to the bank and talk with them. It's nearly three and the bank'll be closed, but we can get in to the manager. We'll take a taxi. It'll kill me to walk in this heat.'

'It would be a tall order, Keelagher trying to get out of the country with more than twenty thousand in cash, wouldn't it?'

'Not as bad as it used to be, Littlejohn. Things are very much easier on that score now. A false bottom, a good one, in a suitcase and Bob's your Uncle. Leaving England, he'd have no trouble at all; entering France... Well... You say they'd a caravan. The French people would be very busy with the caravan, but probably a suitcase would get away with it. Judging from what you say, an ingenuous young couple in their natty new caravan taking an old uncle abroad with them, would hardly be objects of suspicion. Nobody would think of them shunting large quantities of cash about. It's a safe bet.'

Mr. Beddoes, Manager of the Home Counties Bank, in Cornhill, was, as a rule, inaccessible after three o'clock, especially on that day, when he had a golf appointment at Putney. Home Counties Bank v. Hercules Assurance Co. But he sat up and clutched his throat at the sight of Flight's card. Fraud Squad, by gad! He thought of the cash, now being packed away in the vaults, and of the books, now being electrically balanced and wondered which of the staff was the serpent in his bosom.

'Send him in,' he said faintly after taking a tot of the brandy which he kept by him in case certain customers were overcome by his decisions.

Flight and Littlejohn entered. At the sight of Littlejohn, Mr. Beddoes was comforted. He knew Littlejohn and felt he'd a friend at court who would see him through.

'Good afternoon. What about a cup of tea?'

The tea quickly arrived and they began to talk. Flight did most of the talking, referring now and then to the beer-card which he put in his inside pocket, a pocket of the poacher's variety perhaps now and then used for carrying ledgers here and there.

'I understand that the stockbroking firm of Keelagher and Heller keep their accounts with you, Mr. Beddoes.'

'They do. But I know you'll understand, Mr. Flight, that I'm in no position to divulge any information without an order of the Court.'

'I'm well aware of that, sir. Just let's talk, however, and if I overstep the mark, you'll have to pull me up. I can assure you that anything you tell us will be treated in the strictest confidence. You understand that, don't you? I speak with the full weight and integrity of Scotland Yard behind me.'

The thought of such weight almost overcame Mr. Beddoes. He said he fully understood.

'Keelagher and Heller perhaps from time to time enjoyed overdrafts with you?'

Mr. Beddoes smiled, in spite of the gravity of the interview. He was a man with a sense of humour.

'One could hardly say *enjoyed*. The commotion about interest rates and security which occurred every time they borrowed from us was more of a torment. However, they did overdraw quite frequently. In confidence, that is.'

'Secured by the partners?'

'Yes.'

'You look uneasy, Mr. Beddoes. I'll try to skate clear of confidential details. This is a murder case, you know. We're trying to find out who killed George Keelagher. Is that clear?'

'Quite; and I wish to help all I can within the bounds of professional secrecy. Go on.'

'What was the nature of the security?'

'I shall have to take some time explaining that. First, the Keelagher family had formed an investment trust. It is quite a familiar way, as you'll know.'

'I certainly do.'

'Mr. George, Miss Lucy and one or two others, including Mr. Heller, had shares in this trust. You see, originally, the Keelaghers pooled much of their resources in the trust and with the funds invested in a number of undertakings. The trust owned shares in such undertakings and drew the dividends, but the Keelaghers owned the trust and held the shares of it. The trust paid dividends from its investment income. Do you follow? It was like one of the many unit trusts or investments companies which are so popular with the public nowadays. In the case of the Keelagher Trust, there was a certain income tax angle which caused them to create it.'

'You're telling me,' said Flight and smacked his lips.

Mr. Beddoes looked alarmed.

'There's nothing wrong, is there? I mean... the bank...'

'No, sir. Not as far as we're aware. Mr. George Keelagher, we believe, took a lot of money abroad with him before he met his death. We're trying to trace it.'

'Ah. You mean the cash he took from the firm when he gave up his partnership.'

'So, instead of quoted investments, the partners deposited the shares of the trust as security?'

'That's right. Such shares are very valuable. There is behind them, all the investments of the trust, which are held here for custody. We thus had full knowledge of what was going on. We regarded the trust shares as first class.'

'But unquoted on the Stock Exchange? It was a private trust?'

'Yes. But all the holders were obviously wealthy. The firm didn't borrow very extensively. We regarded ourselves as quite safe.'

'Who were the shareholders in the investment trust?'

'That will be very confidential. It concerns only the holders and...'

'I promised you when we came that we would not divulge anything you told us without covering you officially.'

'I agree. Mr. George Keelagher, Miss Lucy Keelagher, Mr. James Keelagher, Mr. Waldo Keelagher and Mr. Herbert Heller... They're the main shareholders. There are other minor ones of no real account.'

'Is Mr. Heller heavily in it?'

'Much less than Mr. George and Miss Lucy, who are by far the main shareholders.'

Flight turned to Littlejohn.

'You understand what we're getting at. It's briefly this. Instead of investing their own money individually, the Keelagher group of people have pooled it in the Keelagher Trust, which, in turn, has invested the funds in its name. It has issued receipts for the separate monies called Share Certificates, draws the dividends from the companies in which it has invested, and pays the bulk of them out to its shareholders, the Keelaghers.'

'I see.'

'Now, Mr. Beddoes, could you tell me the total share capital of the Keelagher Trust?'

'Yes. One hundred thousand pounds in £1 shares. It has been at that figure for about twenty years. Now, a £1 share of the Trust is worth at least £5. Due to capital growth, of course.'

'I quite see that. Have you a list of the shareholders?'

'Yes. I must remind you that this is a private company and the information is strictly confidential. However, if it is helping to capture the murderer of Mr. George Keelagher, I'll take a chance.'

'I won't let you down, sir.'

Mr. Beddoes consulted a private file which he kept in his personal safe in the corner of the room.

'The shares are held as follows:

1.	George Keelagher	25,000
2.	Lucy Alice Keelagher	25,000
3.	James Emerson Keelagher and Ralph Waldo Keelagher	20,000
4.	Herbert Henry Heller	20,000
5–9.	Sundry Holdings in five names	10,000
		100,000 shares

'The holding of 20,000 in the names of James and Waldo Keelagher is not their own property but that of the Percival Potter Keelagher Trust. It was created by their grandfather's will and Mr. George and Miss Lucy take the income equally until their deaths. Then the whole reverts equally to James and Waldo.'

'Have you there a list of the share certificates?'

'I have.'

'Nine, in all, have been issued?'

'Yes. They are numbered One to Nine. No more.'

'Some of them are charged to your bank as security.'

'Yes, as I said. Mr. George and Mr. Heller jointly deposited them as security for their firm's borrowing from us.'

'Certificates Numbered One and Four.'

'Quite correct.'

Mr. Beddoes was looking bewildered. He wondered how much more Superintendent Flight was wanting to know and what he was going to do with all the information.

'Is that all?

'One more question. Who is the secretary of the Keelagher Trust?'

'Mr. Heller.'

'For how long has he been secretary?'

'Oh...I'd say since the late Mr. P. P. Keelagher died. Mr. George was secretary until then, when he turned it over to Mr. Heller, who wasn't even a partner in the firm then, but their chief clerk.'

'Does Mr. Heller bank with you?'

'No. He said he didn't like the idea of banking with the same bank as the firm. It might lead to some confusion. His account is with the City and Counties Bank in Gracechurch Street.'

'Well, I think that's all, Mr. Beddoes, and we're very much obliged by your ready assistance. Thank you for the tea. It's cooled me down very nicely. You may depend on our not abusing your frank help and rest assured that you've greatly speeded up the solution of the Keelagher case.'

'I hope so.'

'Hope we haven't kept you too long.'

'Oh, no ...'

Mr. Beddoes imagined the Chairman of the Hercules Assurance waiting for him at the bar of the Putney Club, slowly consuming whisky and looking at his watch every minute. Perhaps if it made him a little unsteady, he might prove less formidable on the course.

'Good afternoon, gentlemen.'

The clocks were striking half-past four.

'I wonder if the manager of the City and Counties has gone home yet. Poor old Beddoes obviously had a golf appointment. He kept looking at the clock and eyeing his golf-bag in one corner. Let's try ...'

They turned into Gracechurch Street and entered by a sort of postern gate let in the huge walls of the City and Counties Bank. The messenger on duty was surprised. The newcomers didn't look like tycoons. He asked them rather aggressively what they wanted as the bank had been closed for almost two hours.

'What is your manager's name?'

'Mr. Greeley. He has an appointment and is not available.'

Superintendent Flight handed the man his card.

'Take that to him, please.'

The man with the large brass buttons looked down his nose at it, after putting on a pair of spectacles.

'Crikey! Just a moment, sir.'

Mr. Greeley had an appointment, it was true. With his wife. They were going to the theatre and she had chosen to dine with him at his club, which admitted ladies to certain parts of the precincts after five. Mrs. Greeley wore the trousers in their partnership and he knew she would bully him in front of his fellow members. It wasn't dignified. He didn't like it. He looked that way, too, when Littlejohn and Flight entered. He stood on the hearthrug frowning heavily at the portrait of Mr. John William Rawlinson, in whose draper's shop in Wolverhampton had started a small bank which had ended up as the massive City and Counties group.

'You're late. I've an appointment at any moment,' said Mr. Greeley, taking snuff and disposing of it with a red silk handkerchief. Actually, his stomach was turning over, but he was putting on a bold front. Like Mr. Beddoes, he was wondering *what* it was and *who* it was.

Mr. Greeley also knew Littlejohn, who'd once done him a good turn by recovering the proceeds of a hold-up at a small branch where Mr. Greeley had started his managerial career. If it hadn't been for Littlejohn, he certainly wouldn't now have been preening himself on the managerial rug of the best branch in their group. He felt a rush of gratitude and wrung Littlejohn's hand warmly.

'Glad to see you again.'

He wasn't sure that was true, but he'd see.

Littlejohn introduced Flight this time. Mr. Greeley had heard of Flight, too. He turned dark red.

'What is it?' he said anxiously.

'I'll come to the point, sir. It won't take long. Does Mr. Herbert Heller bank with you?'

Ha! So that was it. Mr. Greeley's guard went up.

'Yes.'

'Has he an overdraft?'

Mr. Greeley almost collapsed.

'Really! That's hardly a question I can answer, Flight. Such a matter lies merely between banker and customer. We don't divulge those things.'

Mr. Flight went on to tell Mr. Greeley what he'd told Mr. Beddoes. The murder of George Keelagher, the difficulties of obtaining information about the late unhappy George and his affairs. The awkwardness of obtaining Court Orders during an investigation, in which the slightest breath of what was going on might startle the murderer and cause him to flee or do something even more bloodthirsty.

Littlejohn intervened and added his weight to Flight's humble pleas. Mr Greeley felt that he owed Littlejohn a debt and swore him to secrecy.

'If I divulge this without the usual legal cover, it's as good as my job is worth. You'll keep it to yourselves and, if you wish to make use of the information, call again fortified with full powers?'

'Agreed.'

'Mr. Heller is overdrawn here.'

They knew it already after all the palaver, but there were more difficult fences to clear.

'Substantially?'

'Well, well. You're pushing me hard, gentlemen. Still, it's the police and in the public interest, I suppose. No judge would condemn me for co-operating. Yes; substantially. And that's my last word.'

Flight took up his hat and smiled.

'We're very grateful to you, Mr. Greeley, and we'll respect your confidence. By the way, one little innocuous detail. How is the loan secured? By shares? I suppose it is, seeing Mr. Heller's a stockbroker.'

'That is right.'

'Quoted securities?'

Mr. Greeley paused.

'I can't tell you that. I've already said enough.'

Flight shrugged. He took a chance.

'We know what the security is. It's a share certificate for 20,000 £1 shares in the Keelagher Trust, isn't it? The shares are roughly worth £5 for each £1 share.'

Mr. Greeley's eyes stood out.

'Why ask me if you know it all? You have been talking to Mr. Heller and are merely confirming the information he's given you? I can't see how it all squares up with a murder investigation unless...'

His eyes popped wider.

'Surely you don't suspect Heller. It's preposterous.'

'Just routine, sir.'

'Routine, eh? You fellows work hard, don't you? If this is mere routine what will a special investigation be like?'

'Another question, sir.'

Mr. Greeley raised his eyes to heaven and then shook his head in a gesture of despair.

'Ask it. Whether you get an answer or not is another matter.'

'May I suggest that the Keelagher Trust certificate lodged with you is Number *Four*?'

'At last! A question I can't answer. All the same, your guess is interesting. It won't do any harm to confirm it, if we can. It will be in our Security Register. If the books haven't been put away and the vault locked, we can verify it.'

Mr. Greeley began to look in better shape. He smiled to himself. Mrs. Greeley would already have arrived at the bank and been told that her husband was in conference. The longer such conference lasted, the shorter the time they'd spend over dinner at the club. That would shorten

Mr. Greeley's ordeal there; he wouldn't have to sit for so long with his fellow members watching his wife bullying him. He buoyantly flipped up a switch on his desk.

'Yes, sir?' said a voice which seemed to come from the top drawer of the desk itself.

'Bannister?'

'Yes, sir.'

'Are the books away?'

'Yes, sir. Anything I can do, sir?'

'Is the vault closed?'

'No, sir. The Inspectors are checking the cash.'

'Good! Bring me Security Register Ha to Ho.'

It sounded a very cordial sort of ledger!

In a very short time a senior clerk arrived lugging a metal-bound loose-leaf ledger with the greetings Ha-Ho inscribed on its back in letters of gold.

'Turn up Herbert Heller's page, Mr. Bannister.'

It didn't take long. There was Mr. Heller's page with the Keelagher Trust security inscribed on it. Nothing more. Perhaps it was all he had in the world.

The recorded share certificate was Number Four.

'By gad! You're right. How did you know?'

Bannister stood cheerfully there, although he hadn't a clue what the whole rigmarole was about. He was taking his girl out as soon as work was finished, and he felt good about it.

'Right, Bannister. That will be all, thank you.'

Bannister staggered away with Ha-Ho.

'I'm sorry, Mr. Greeley, but I must now make another request.'

By this time, Mr. Greeley was in a fatalistic mood of expecting anything. His Uncle Arnold, one-time professor of philosophy in a minor university, had often told

him, "Arnold; what is, *is,* and what has to be, has to be."
Mr. Greeley felt like that now. Good old Uncle Arnold! His
godfather!! If Flight had asked to check all the cash, he
wouldn't have been surprised.

'What is it?'

'May I be allowed to see share certificate No. 4?'

'Really? What good is all this doing? You *know* it is No.
4; I know it's No. 4; Littlejohn knows it's No. 4. Can't you
believe your own eyes or our records?'

'May I see it?'

'Very well. Highly irregular and inconvenient. But I
might as well be hanged for a sheep as a lamb.'

Bannister again.

Bannister didn't seem to mind. He ran here and there,
assembling, by now, belated officials and marching them off
with keys at the ready to find the certificate in the Ha-Ho
cabinet.

'What's cooking, Banny?' asked one of the clerks as they
flipped their fingers through the piles of security and eventually unearthed the required document.

'I don't know. The boss is in a regular flap. The two
chaps in his room are detectives the head messenger says.
That's a blow. I wonder if old Greeley's been staging a hold-
up in a rival bank, or else been fiddling our own books. To
add to the strain, Mrs. G's in the waiting-room raising Cain.
It seems they're going to the theatre when the Scotland Yard
men have finished with our Arnold. She'll murder him ...'

When the certificate arrived, Flight carefully examined
it under his pocket glass. In handwriting it certified that Mr.
Herbert Henry Heller was the owner of 20,000 shares in the
said company, and it was sealed on behalf of the company
by George Keelagher, a Director, "on this the 27th day of
October, 1945."

'Satisfied?'

'Quite. And very many thanks for your help, sir.'

'I hope there's nothing wrong.'

'I can't tell you at this stage, sir. But we'll keep in touch with you.'

'But surely... I've been very forthcoming. Can't you be the same...? In confidence, of course.'

'I can't say more than that it has helped us in investigating the murder of Mr. Keelagher. As soon as I'm able to tell you all about it, I'll call and do so... Or, at least, Superintendent Littlejohn, in charge of the case, will let you know. I don't even know myself yet where we are in the matter.'

In this uncertain and highly-strung state, they had to leave Mr. Greeley to make his peace with his wife.

Flight was much more communicative to Littlejohn as they left the City.

'Let's go and get a cup of tea. Beer only makes me sweat more. Tea's the thing.'

They descended to another cellar and ordered tea and toasted muffins, of which Flight consumed large quantities every day. Over the meal, he opened up on the case again.

'Two certificates numbered Four, for 20,000 shares apiece. There can't be *two* genuine ones. The capital is authorised at 100,000 shares. The extra number Four would increase the total to 120,000, which isn't legal. The certificate held by Greeley on Heller's account is the red flag. You follow?'

'I think I do. Heller is the secretary of the Trust and presumably controls the stock of blank share certificates and the seal of the company. To secure his overdraft, he illegally issued an extra certificate. He must have forged George Keelagher's signature, too.'

'He did. He wrote out the certificate in his own hand and then, using a different pen and ink of another colour, he forged George Keelagher's name on the document. I'm a bit of an expert on forgeries after all this time and I'll bet a fiver that our handwriting blokes confirm my views.'

'A fiver! You are being rash, Horace.'

'Anything you like, then. I wonder if Heller is still at the office?'

It had just struck six and the bells of one of the City churches were playing '*There's no Luck about the House.*'

Fortunately the old song hadn't that day applied to the Stock Exchange. Steels and Oils had risen phenomenally, the numbers of markings had been considerable, and Keelagher and Heller were working overtime at full steam.

Nevertheless, the staff were surprised at the arrival of visitors at that late hour. They thought at first that they were naïve clients up from the country to claim their profits for the day in cash.

'This is your affair, now, Littlejohn,' Flight had told him. Littlejohn therefore sent in his card to Heller, and asked if he might see him for a few minutes.

When the card and the request were placed before Mr. Heller, he ran to the lavatory and locked himself in.

After a wait of half-an-hour, Littlejohn enquired what was keeping Mr. Heller.

The clerk was embarrassed and amused at the same time.

'Well?'

'I think he's in the lavatory.'

'All this time?'

'Yes. He mustn't be well.'

'Where is the place?'

'It's a private one through the other door of his room.'

'Show us.'

'But...'

'Show us...'

They had to break-in the door and there they found Mr. Heller on the floor, half conscious, feeding himself mechanically with tablets from a bottle. He'd apparently consumed more than fifty tablets of aspirin, all without a drink!

They rushed him off to Charing Cross Hospital, where Mr. Heller was appropriately and expertly dealt with under feeble protests and with many lamentations.

Finally, he fell in a troubled sleep, with a policeman outside the room.

Next morning, Mr. Heller tried to jump through the window. He was a most persistent little man. The custodian bobby was very exasperated and told Mr. Heller what he'd do to him if he tried it again.

When Littlejohn arrived at the hospital, Mr. Heller seemed resigned to his fate and was asking the bobby in charge of him what it was like in prison these days and what exactly were the circumstances in which a murderer was hanged.

He confessed to Littlejohn right away, that it was he who had murdered George Keelagher.

CHAPTER THIRTEEN
UNWELCOME ALIBI

Before Leaving for the hospital, Littlejohn and Cromwell fully discussed the developments of the case, especially in the light of what Flight's help had revealed.

It looked very much as if Heller had been blackmailed by his partner, Keelagher, for years and, pushed too far, had decided to make an end of it. How the matter tied-up with the forged share certificate and Keelagher's decision to leave England and live in a monastery in Canada, was still a mystery.

'However, let's make sure of the details we do know, Cromwell. We'd better go into the matter of Heller's alibi.'

Smiles, Keelagher's junior partner, had definitely stated that Heller was regularly at the office on every working day at well before ten o'clock. If this were true on the morning of August 8th, when Keelagher met his death, Heller was in the clear.

James Keelagher had a watertight alibi. At least half a dozen of his colleagues in the pepper trade had seen him at nine-thirty on the morning of the crime. They had been forming a syndicate to corner the market and had met before the exchange opened for the day.

The principal suspects, short of some random intruder, who happened to be on the road and saw Keelagher prowling round the caravan site and killed him for his cash, or some other trivial purpose, were Waldo, James, Heller, Richley and possibly Miss Lucy or Mrs. Benson.

Miss Lucy, Richley and Benson gave each other alibis. They'd all been together for the day from breakfast time and Richley had an additional sponsor in the television man who, that day, had made *Pontresina* his first port of call to repair Richley's set.

James was in the clear. There remained Waldo and Heller. If Smiles stuck to his story about Heller's punctual and regular appearance at the office, it looked as if Waldo would be very much in the queer.

'Go and talk to Smiles again, old chap, and see if you can't make a hole in his persistence. I'm off to the hospital to see how Heller is getting along.'

Littlejohn lit his pipe and was just enjoying it in the early morning freshness, when he had to knock it out again as he entered Charing Cross Hospital.

They told him about Heller's attempt to throw himself through the window.

'He's a very determined man. He seems to want to die and to be attracted by the sticky ways of doing it.'

Heller looked a sorry sight, in bed, out of favour with the staff for causing a commotion, haggard and strained from his efforts with the aspirin on the night before and his early morning performance in front of the window overlooking the Strand.

He was nothing to be proud of at the best of times. Small, shrivelled, drawn with the perpetual worry of a profession for which he was naturally unsuited, unlucky in love and in stocks and shares, he seemed to have little for which to thank the gods. Finally, he had been bullied and eternally harassed by Keelagher, his dominating partner. He had perhaps killed him and then, finding himself unable to cope without Keelagher and his domineering, had seen so little in life that he wished to throw it away.

Heller was like a corpse already; waxen, drawn in the face, still-featured. And yet, as Littlejohn looked at him, he noted the bright eyes, like those of a snake, glittering with some purpose. Probably a determination to try death again once he was free.

'Good morning, Mr. Heller. How are you feeling?'

'It's you again, is it? What do you want?'

Littlejohn asked the attendant constable to wait outside, but had more difficulty in persuading the presiding sister to leave them alone.

'He's had a sedative and shouldn't be bothered with talking. He really ought to be kept quiet for at least three or four days.'

It doesn't seem to matter that Heller was involved in an unsolved murder and that the information he might give was urgently needed. To sister, Heller was a *Case* and one to be treated in a world apart from the troubles and rough-houses of the everyday life outside the hospital. Mr. Heller was 'bedded' and in that condition he and everybody else, including the police, would behave themselves and do as they were told.

'Has the doctor seen him?'

'Of course.'

'What did he say?'

'You'd better ask him. He's on the wards and will soon be calling here. He'll say the same as me.'

A little, tight-lipped, dedicated girl, as loyal and as duti-ful as a good soldier, she almost put Littlejohn out of coun-tenance. It was Heller who made her change her mind.

'Nurse!'

He screeched it so loudly that sister and Littlejohn jumped.

'Nurse! I've something important to tell him. You'd better let me talk to him. Otherwise, I won't eat, I won't sleep, I'll keep ringing the bell till you're sick of the sound of it, and, at the first chance, I'll try to jump through the window again. I'll ...'

She tried to give him a sedative and he knocked the glass from her hand, and when she finally produced a hypodermic, he swore he'd disarm her and stab her with it.

In the middle of it all, the consultant arrived, followed by a band of students, whom he dismissed to the other side of the door when he found what was going on.

'You'd better allow them ten minutes together, sister. Otherwise, the patient will need physical force to quieten him. Leave them. Perhaps if Mr. Heller opens his heart to someone, it will do him good.'

As soon as they were alone, Heller spoke.

'I want to tell you right away that I killed George Keelagher. I'd had enough of him and could stand it no longer.'

He pulled himself up in his bed and suddenly grew animated.

'Excuse me, sir. You needn't make a statement if you don't wish. But I must warn you that anything you say may be used in evidence. It is my duty to tell you that, although there is nobody present to confirm what you are going to tell me.'

Heller waved his arms about.

'Don't waste time. Those nurses and doctors will be back again before I've finished what I have to say. You don't think I'd waste my breath if I wasn't prepared to sign a statement later.'

'Very well, Mr. Heller.'

'It's a long story and goes back a long way. I'm sixty now and served with Keelaghers for forty-five years. I joined them as a junior clerk and worked my way up, if you can call it *up*. Now I know it was *down*. I'd a choice between Keelaghers' and Knightons', the solicitors. Knightons' told me I could never hope to be more than a managing clerk. George Keelagher, then a young man, said that if I behaved myself and did well, I'd probably be a partner one day. I am a partner now. He was right. And *what* a partner!'

He angrily flapped about among the bedclothes, disordering his bed, trying to make himself comfortable again so that he could gesticulate as he spoke. He seemed a nervous wreck.

'I gradually made progress at Keelaghers' and rose to be Mr. Keelagher senior's clerk. When he retired, I became Mr. George's private secretary, served them on the floor of the House, gave my life to them. Then, one day, when I was at Mr. Keelagher's home, I met Miss Lucy...'

He took a drink from a glass of what looked like barley water and Littlejohn watched the progress of the liquid down his scraggy throat, agitating his large Adam's apple.

'You won't think it possible, I know, but you can please yourself whether or not you believe me. I don't care. But we fell in love with one another. She mustn't have had much choice, picking me, but there it was. It was the best thing in my life. But I was always unlucky. It soon ended. I mentioned it to Mr. George and asked if I might pay attentions to her. He laughed and said, of course. Then, in that diabolical way he had, he added, but it wouldn't do for me to marry the boss's sister and me only a clerk in the office. I'd better become a partner. I was stunned. I thought that, at last, my luck had changed. But there was a fly in the ointment. There always was.'

He sank back, overcome by his thoughts and despair. He spoke again, rolling his head from side to side. It seemed to have grown loose, like that of a rag doll.

'Do you know what he said? He said, had I any money to invest in the firm to merit the partnership? You'd have thought that after all my years of faithful service to him and his father, they'd have made me a present of it. But no. Do you know how much George Keelagher wanted to smooth the way for my marrying his sister? Twenty thousand pounds! Twenty thousand!! He knew he might as well have asked for the moon. He said, of course, that would, as a member of the family, entitle me to shares in the Keelagher Trust, which would bring in an income suitable for keeping his sister. I'd saved a bit. Five thousand, about. I asked if that would do as a start and I'd try to pay the rest by degrees. He shook his head, and asked if friends wouldn't help me. He knew I had no friends of that sort. I'd never had time to make any, working as I did all the hours God sent for his blasted firm. He told me to think it over for a few days and he gave me a broad hint that it would be no cash, no Miss Lucy.'

Heller was obviously exhausting himself partly by talking and partly by hatred. His eyes were glazed and he spoke in a monotonous, whining voice now, with few gestures and all the force of his early statement quite spent.

'I was secretary of the Keelagher Trust. The blank share certificates were in my possession as was the seal of the company. Now listen. You're not a business man and this is a bit tricky. About that time there'd been a famous criminal procedure against a financier who issued fraudulent shares in a company and in turning over in my mind what I must do, I thought of it. I'd five thousand pounds in the bank. I went to see the manager. I told him that I was shortly to marry

Miss Lucy Keelagher and as a part of the settlement would receive twenty thousand shares in the family trust. I showed him the balance-sheet and figures of the trust. They were good ones, as the manager agreed. I asked, if I deposited as security the forthcoming shares, he would lend me fifteen thousand pounds. That, with my own savings, would provide the necessary amount for the partnership. I told him that I would be a partner and I suppose he thought that, if he accommodated me, I'd perhaps one day bring him some substantial business, for our firm was a wealthy and progressive one. He agreed.'

Heller took another drink and licked his thin, pale lips.

'I told Mr. George that a friend had arranged to lend me the money. He seemed very surprised, but said he'd stick to his bargain. But there was a snag. The bank wouldn't lend the money to a mere clerk like me without the security and Keelagher wouldn't issue the shares in the Trust without the cash. I daren't tell Keelagher I was borrowing from the bank. I was, for one thing, too proud, and for the other, and much more important, I'd got the idea that somehow he was trying to ruin my plans and my marriage to his sister and, if he knew my plans, would obstruct them. I didn't know what to do. Then, I remembered the fraudulent share matter. I assure you I didn't intend to commit a fraud; just tide myself over...'

They all said that! To them, it was invariably true and they thought it justified what they had done.

'I issued a certificate for 20,000 shares, sealed it, and signed George Keelagher's name to it as a director. That wasn't difficult. I'd worked with the signature for years and had even copied it to amuse myself. I went and deposited the share certificate at the bank, drew the cheque, took it to Keelagher, and said my friend had lent me the money. He authorised and signed another certificate, which I took the precaution to issue with the same number that I'd put on the other one. You see, I intended taking it to the bank and on some excuse, changing it for the forged one and destroying the latter. Well ...'

Heller even smiled grimly, a bitter twisted grin, as though now enjoying the tricks of fate.

'Well ... George Keelagher wasn't to be taken-in that way. He'd already enquired at my bank, from someone he knew there, and found I'd deposited the spurious certificate. As he signed and handed over the real certificate, he just quietly said, "And that, Heller, is a genuine, not a phoney one." I was flabbergasted. But he didn't threaten me with the police. He simply said, I could leave the forged one with my bank as security; nobody would ever know. The real one, I could deposit with the firm's bank against any overdraft. When this was done, I'd nothing left, you see. Nothing. I owed my bank £15,000 against a worthless piece of paper and, if Keelagher cared to draw against the firm's account, he could take up to £20,000 against my genuine certificate which would be sold if the firm didn't repay if the bank called-in their overdraft. To add salt to the wound, I'd to repay my own bank five hundred a year, at least, plus interest on the loan against the false document.'

What a pickle! No wonder Heller was almost round the bend with hate and worry!

'It didn't end there. Keelagher said he could have me put in gaol any time he cared to divulge what I'd done. He'd arranged with my bank to let him know if ever I asked for withdrawal of the forged certificate, by giving them notice that he had a second charge on it. This is the way he blackmailed me through all the years. He didn't ask for money; just obedience. I was his partner in name alone and did just as he told me. Nothing dishonest; just the reminder that he had the whip hand...'

Heller swallowed hard. The next looked like being difficult to tell.

'But there's worse to come. *The* worst. Keelagher said he couldn't allow his sister to marry a crook. Yes; a crook. I must never see her again. I begged him to spare us that. I tried to show him that I hadn't had any evil intentions. Just a matter of convenience. He said he'd call in the police if I ever saw his sister again. He made me write a letter asking her to excuse me. I was to say it had all been a mistake as there was someone else. I did it. I did it!! I should have killed him then and there. Instead, I ruined my own life and happiness and Lucy's as well.'

'Excuse me...You saw Miss Lucy recently and spoke to her?'

'Who told you that? Yes; I did. I made up my mind I'd had enough. I went round to see her. She refused to see me twice. Then I wrote to her, telling her it was urgent and I wouldn't take any liberties with her. I admitted I'd wronged her and wished to explain something she didn't know. She agreed to see me. I told her the whole sorry tale. I asked her to forgive me. She showed me the door. That is all.'

'When and why did you decide to kill Keelagher?'

'It was the last straw that did it. For some time he'd been talking of retiring. He proposed packing everything up and going abroad to live. He said he wanted a bit of peace and quiet and was going to write a book. He was what he called a naturalist in his spare time. It was like him to be interested in the study of revolting insects. He said he was leaving the firm and I could follow him as senior partner. He must have accumulated quite a lot of money from his speculations, although, as far as I could discover recently, had either lost it again or hidden it somewhere. Probably the latter, knowing Keelagher. He wanted more. I thought the twenty thousand he twisted and blackmailed out of me would have been enough to establish me as head. But no; Keelagher wanted more. He'd thought out another of his schemes. The firm's banking account was in credit, but Keelagher had evidently arranged with the manager to overdraw again. He'd taken away all the securities he'd placed as the bank as cover for any borrowing we might need, but had blackmailed me into leaving my certificate in the Keelagher Trust at the bank as security. Now, he came along, said he was going to take £20,000 from the bank as overdraft against my security and leave *me* with the debt. I pleaded with him not to make me penniless. He laughed and said I'd now a chance to show my mettle at speculating and making money. He drew£20,000 in cash from the bank and left me to repay it. I couldn't do a thing about it. The forged certificate was still at my bank and I owed a large sum against it. Keelagher had only to tell my bank that the certificate was a fake and I'd land in gaol. I thought that once Keelagher was out of the way, I'd think out some scheme for putting myself right once and for all. And then I asked myself why he should get away with it every time. All the years I'd suffered from his bullying, blackmail and humiliation. All the money I'd ever had, Keelagher had taken from me. And, finally, instead of having a wife and comfort for my old age, I'd nothing. I was a sort of comic, bad-tempered bachelor with nothing to look forward to...I decided to kill Keelagher and, at least get my £20,000 in cash back.'

The monotonous voice went on and on. There might have been nothing exciting in it for Heller. Just a dull, droning narrative, climbing to a climax which, judging from the hopeless way in which Heller told of it, might easily have been a flop, like everything else in Heller's history.

The sister had been in twice and after seeing the patient comfortable and apparently quiet, had gone, after a disapproving look at Littlejohn.

'Next time I come in, you'll have to go. The patient must get some rest.'

'Keelagher suddenly announced that he was going to the Riviera in his nephew Waldo's caravan. It wasn't difficult to obtain from Waldo the route they were taking and the dates they'd be at certain places. I made up my mind to meet Keelagher at Cannes at a spot in the hills where Waldo, who was always methodical about such things, said they proposed to stay a few days whilst his uncle studied his abominable insects...'

Heller took another drink and pulled himself up in the bed.

'I took the night 'plane and from Nice got a taxi to a spot where I could easily walk from to the site they'd chosen. It was dawn when the 'plane got in and I followed my plan, intending to find the caravan and more or less spy out the land for a convenient meeting when Keelagher was on his own. When I got there, I saw Keelagher outside the caravan, dressed and ready, apparently off to study his insects again. I thought that was my chance. I was sure he'd got the money there with him and hoped to force him to hand it over. There he was and there was my chance. I ran across from the bushes where I was hiding and faced him. He looked surprised. Then he started to laugh at me and taunted me because he said I looked like some kind of lizard running about the place. I had taken my revolver with me and I just pulled it out and shot him. I did it in a fit of rage forgetting I'd still not got the £20,000 back. I was afraid the shot would have wakened someone and I'd be caught in the net. I beat a retreat. Undignified, as usual. I returned on the next 'plane...'

He paused and looked at Littlejohn to see how the story was affecting him.

'If you like to have it typed out, I'll sign it. I suppose you'll arrest me when I can be moved.'

'May I refer to the interview you had with Inspector Cromwell in Mr. Craddock's office, when you very forcibly revealed that George Keelagher had absconded with the £20,000? Do I take it that was an act you put on to stake your claim to the £20,000 in case the police came across it in the course of their enquiries?'

'I couldn't very well at the time tell the whole tale about the blackmail and incriminate myself on the forged certificate count. I hadn't decided then to make a clean breast of the whole affair. So, I sailed as close to the wind as I dared without danger, in trying to get my money back. After all, it was my money. If the police found it, they might easily have turned it over to Keelagher's estate.'

'There are one or two other questions we'll have to settle in due course, Mr. Heller. The revolver, for instance. What kind was it?'

'I don't know. It was an old one we had in the office. I took it as I left to meet Keelagher so that I could threaten him. I threw it in the river near Nice airport.'

'Have you ever been to Nice before?'

'Yes. Several times. When my mother was alive, she often wintered there and I went with her sometimes.'

'Had you ever fired a revolver before?'

'Yes. I was in the Home Guard in the war. I'm tired now. I want to rest...'

Sister was in again; this time followed by Cromwell.

'A gentleman to see Superintendent Littlejohn. And, after that, you will please go. The patient is exhausted. I won't be responsible if...'

'Just another couple of minutes, sister.'

Cromwell had written a statement in his black book. It was from Smiles, Heller's junior partner, concerning the morning Keelagher was killed. Littlejohn read it carefully.

'Mr. Heller, just one more question, if you please.'

'Be quick then and get it over. I want to sleep now that I've got what I told you off my chest.'

'Your clothes are here?'

'Yes. Why? You're not taking those, are you, to stop me running away? I give you my word I'll...'

'Your railway season ticket from Chislehurst is in the pocket?'

'Yes. What good is that going to do?'

Littlejohn opened the wardrobe in the corner and took out a wallet from an inside pocket of the jacket hanging there. There was a first-class season ticket inside it. Littlejohn examined it.

'Mr. Heller, your season ticket is dated August 9th...'

'Well...?'

'On August 8th, you travelled to Cannon Street station from Chislehurst with your partner, Mr. Smiles, who also lives there. He swears this was the case and remembers it particularly, because as you showed your season ticket at the barriers, you remarked to him, "My season ticket expires tonight; remind me to order a new one for tomorrow." At the time you say you were in the South of France, you were actually travelling to London on your usual morning train. There were others, as well as Mr. Smiles, who can testify the same. I think the story of how you actually killed Keelagher was made-up from details you've obtained from the newspapers, which are now full of the case.'

Heller turned his face to the wall and refused to speak again.

Chapter Fourteen
The Wanderer

When Littlejohn and Cromwell arrived at Metropolitan Terrace again there was a van standing at the door of the Richleys' home and two men were moving a harmonium from it and carrying it indoors. Richley was in the offing directing operations.

'You again! You've arrived at an inconvenient time. As you see, we're busy. It won't take long ...'

Had the men with the organ not been in a hurry, he would probably have said a lot more. He seemed nervous and prone to chatter to disguise his uneasiness.

'Nice to have one's own home in which to house one's belongings. This instrument has been at my brother's for many years. Awkward havin' to go to Fulham every time I wished to practise or entertain myself. Now I've got it on the spot and can play when I wish without incommoding anyone.'

Littlejohn wondered what the neighbours would have to say to the regular sound of hymns in the district. He was sure they would be hymns.

'I'd like a few words with you again. It won't take long.'

The men were emerging. They hung round a bit for the price of a pint of beer apiece, but as Richley didn't seem to react, went on their way disgustedly.

Richley conducted the detectives to the room they'd been in before. The furniture had been shunted about to accommodate the harmonium and it looked a bit like a repository.

'Sit down, if you please. As I said before ...'

'You will remember, Mr. Richley, that I asked you for particulars of what went on at *Pontresina* on August 8th, the day Mr. Keelagher was murdered. You stated that you, Mrs. Richley, and Miss Lucy had been about the place from early morning until evening, with the exception of a brief shopping excursion by your wife. Was that true?'

At first, Richley looked ready to argue violently about it. Then he changed his tack and looked pained.

'I'm surprised at you, sir. Doubting my word. I'm not in the 'abit of lying, Superintendent. I told you the truth as far as I knew it.'

'And what does that qualification mean? *As far as you knew it?*'

'I was not Miss Lucy's personal servant, sir. Mrs. Richley looked after her. I told you what Mrs. Richley had told me.'

'We'd better have Mrs. Richley in, then. Is she at home?'

'She is. I'll bring her in if you wish. But I fail to see why you want to bother her. She was hardly likely to lie to *me*, was she?'

He cast his head in the air as though defying them to prove otherwise, and made for the door. As usual, his wife was behind it, looking as though she had walked a long way and had just fetched-up on the threshold.

'I was wondering if you would like a cup of tea after your struggle with the organ ...'

''armonium, my love. No. Not just at present. We're busy. The police are here again. They wish to see you.'

'About Mr Keelagher?'

'Something to that effect. Come inside.'

She looked hot and flustered and as uncomfortable as her husband had been.

'Good afternoon, gentlemen. I hope you're both well.'

'Never mind the courtesies, my dear. We've a busy time in front of us and we've the place to straighten up after the policemen have left. Would you two gentlemen now mind telling Mrs. Richley why you have called?'

Littlejohn told Mrs. Richley what he'd already said to her husband and Richley stood puffing and blowing beside her, ready to give battle on her behalf if she needed him.

'... Did you tell Mr. Richley all that happened on the day in question?'

The woman turned pale and started to finger a large cameo brooch which held the collar of her dress together. The projecting pin pricked her finger and drew a small drop of blood but she didn't seem to notice it. She looked questioningly at Richley.

'Tell them, my dear. Have no fear. You told the truth and that is its own protection.'

He closed his eyes unctuously and then opened them again.

'I didn't exactly. I mean, I didn't tell a lie, but I didn't tell you everything.'

'I am surprised. You'd better tell me and the policemen now, then, my dear. I'm sure you forgot it. It wouldn't be like you...'

'It was Miss Lucy. She wasn't well on the day before Mr. George passed-on. It must have been a premonition. She went to bed that night and took her milk with her. She also took a flask of hot milk and said she wasn't to be disturbed next morning. She was tired and would sleep till noon. She forbade me to disturb her till she rang for me. She said I wasn't to tell you, or Margaret, as you'd only get anxious and make a fuss. I left her quiet ...'

'You mean to tell me, Mrs. Richley, that an elderly ailing woman like Miss Lucy was left in her room from – what time was it? – ten o'clock one night until noon of the next day without your even enquiring if she was all right, at least, the following morning?'

'She locked herself in her room and ...'

'I want the truth, Mrs. Richley. I know a good servant like you would have, at least, tapped on the door early the next day and asked how she was. Did you?'

Mrs. Richley was flustered and the tears began to gather.

'I didn't do anythin' wrong, sir. She asked me not to say anything.'

'You'd better tell us exactly what happened then?'

Richley gave her a forgiving look and patted her on the back to show he was on her side.

'Tell him.'

'After she'd gone to bed, I thought it funny. So, before I turned-in for sleep, I went to her room, knocked, and asked if she was all right. The door was locked, which was unusual. She usually left it loose, so I could get in the next morning and give her her cup of tea. She said she was all right and I was not to disturb her till she rang next day. We said goodnight and I went to bed. Next morning, I couldn't feel happy till I'd seen that she was all right again. I let her sleep till nearly half-past nine and then I tried the door. It was still locked. I knocked and there was no answer. With a bit of jiggling, the key from the room across the passage would unlock Miss Lucy's door. We'd used it before when she lost her own key and we wanted to lock the room when the workmen were in. She kept her jewellery in a drawer there, you see.'

Richley couldn't wait for explanations. He was straining to hear the rest.

'Go on, my dear. We're all waiting for you.'

'When I got the door open, she wasn't inside. The bed had been slept in and she'd drunk the hot milk from her flask. I looked round and found she'd dressed herself and, as her outdoor clothes, bag, and umbrella weren't there, I assumed she'd gone out.'

'And you mentioned it to nobody?'

'She'd asked me not to tell Richley or the girl. So, I thought I'd keep it quiet for an hour or two. I didn't wish to make a fuss about it, because she didn't like a fuss. I said to myself, I'd wait a little while before I told anybody. She might have gone for a walk or to visit a friend. I waited till three o'clock. Then I went to her room to see if she'd taken her case with her. She was in the room, sitting there in the armchair, resting herself.'

'And...?'

'" I thought I told you not to disturb me, Benson," she said. I told her what I'd done and how anxious I'd been and, believe it or not, she thanked me and even kissed me. I don't know where she'd been or how long she'd been there. She was exhausted. Whatever it was, it took it out of her. She's never been the same since. Her heart isn't good and if she'd overdone it, she was taking a great risk.'

'What did she say, exactly, when you found her there?'

'Just that nobody was to know. She didn't want the doctor to start fussing about it. But she said she'd been suddenly taken with a wish to see London and the park again and had just dressed, taken a bus, sat in the park, eaten a poached egg at a café, and was now ready for bed. It's a wonder it didn't kill her.'

'And you thought it best not to tell us in view of your instructions?'

'Yes. With Miss Lucy giving orders and then wandering off and Richley and you, Mr. Cromwell, asking me exactly what she'd done that day, I was between the devil and the deep sea. I thought I'd better do as Miss Lucy said.'

'Did she return by taxi or bus?'

'I didn't see her come in, you see. She came back as quietly and as secretly as she'd gone. She just wandered off and then wandered back without a soul seeing her.'

'Very well, Mrs. Richley. Thank you. I don't think much harm has been done, but, in future, just remember the police come first in a case like this.'

They left Richley and his wife to sort it out the best they could.

'Now Cromwell, we've got to find out where Miss Lucy spent the morning of August 8th. Any ideas?'

'Taxis?'

'That's it. We may as well get at it right away. There won't be a great number of taxi owners in Great Missenden.'

They drove off in the police car and at Great Missenden police station looked up the list of taxi owners and started to telephone. At the sixth attempt a driver called Stanley Torment said he thought he was their man. They asked him to call at the police station for a chat.

Stanley looked anything but a torment when he arrived. Fat, through sitting all day, cheerful and man-of-the-world through studying the characters and capers of those he drove here and there mostly, as he expressed it, "on futile errands", he said that on the night of August 7th, a lady had rung him up, "from a 'phone kiosk judging from the rattle that went on before she got connected." She asked him to pick her up at the corner of Brill Road and Culleys Lane. He'd never seen her before.

'But what struck me as funny was, that she didn't want anybody to reckernise her again. It was dark, see, and she kept her head turned as much as she could. But to cap everythin', she wore a veil, like the old heroines in the mellydramas...'

Littlejohn felt full of compassion. Miss Lucy, out on a dangerous errand, educated for such enterprises by omnivorous crime reading, ended by concealing her identity in a Victorian dark veil. The very thing to make her remembered!

'It was a big job. She paid in advance. Both ways. I don't know what she was really up-to, but she said she wanted to go to Manchester by 'plane to see her sick sister and I was to take her to Heathrow airport. Her money was good and jobs of that sort aren't easy come-by. I took her.'

'You said both ways. Did she book you for the return trip?'

'That's right. Heathrow again at noon the followin' day; back to the same corner. Same veil, except that I got a better look at 'er in daylight. She was quite old and when she came back, she must 'ave had some bad news of her sister. She looked properly done-in. Could hardly climb in the cab. "You not so well, lady?" I asks 'er, and she thanks me very polite, like, for my enquiry, but she's quite all right but a bit tired through bein' up all night. As well she might be. She was a lady. Spoke and behaved different from most fares nowadays. She gave me a good tip and I asks her if I couldn't take 'er right home, as she didn't look up to walking even round the next corner. But, no, she said she'd manage nicely, thank you.'

'Was she carrying a bag?'

'Only a handbag. Black and a bit outsize, like they used to carry in the old days.'

'Well, thank you, Mr. Torment. You've been a big help.'

'And thank you, too. I hope nobody's done her harm. These days, it's the fashion to pick on such nice old ladies and do them violence.'

'No. She's safe and sound enough.'

Littlejohn telephoned to the Sûreté at Nice and asked for Dorange. The Inspector was in his office and asked when Littlejohn would be back.

'Before long, now.'

'Have you had any luck?'

Luck! Littlejohn felt sick at the thought of what he had to do before the case was finally settled and they could set Waldo free again.

'I hope it will be ended before tomorrow. I'll come over to see you right away, then, and square-up matters at your end. Meanwhile, how are Waldo Keelagher and his wife?'

'Still under house arrest, but the examining magistrate, Claudius, has threatened that if there is no progress by tomorrow, he'll arrest them officially and commence formal proceedings. You need any help?'

'Yes. Here is a description of a lady who visited Nice briefly on the night before Keelagher died and remained there until before ten on the morning of the crime ...'

He thereupon gave Dorange a full description of Miss Lucy and told him she had travelled from London to Nice and back by 'plane.

'She left her home outside London for the airport by taxi and when she returned the same taxi picked her up. She may have done the same thing at Nice. Could you enquire there of the taximen if they picked-up anyone from the night 'plane from London answering the description?'

'Certainly. Where do I ring you back?'

'Scotland Yard, please.'

Dorange was a rapid operator.

By the time they reached The Yard from Great Missenden the reply was through.

The person described had taken a taxi to Mandelieu, about five miles from the scene of the crime, paid him to await her return, and joined him again two hours later. Then he'd driven her back to Nice airport and she'd caught the next London 'plane. The taxi driver had seen her board the 'plane himself, as he'd taken a drink in the airport. One couldn't fail to recognise her. She looked like somebody out of the last century. She'd worn a black veil.

Miss Lucy Keelagher must have walked all the way from Mandelieu to the scene of the crime.

She was quite a woman, Miss Lucy.

CHAPTER FIFTEEN
AN END TO WICKEDNESS

M iss Lucy Keelagher had just taken tea when Littlejohn and Cromwell arrived at *Pontresina*. She invited them to have a cup, but they declined, saying they were pressed for time. She looked hard at them. This was unusual, especially for Cromwell who had always seemed to enjoy her hospitality before.

The German maid, Margaret, seemed to have taken charge of the place and of Miss Lucy, as well. The agency had supplied a man and his wife to take, if suitable, the places of the Richleys. A little nondescript fellow, with pale cheeks and a small moustache, and his wife, large, billowy and obviously the boss of the pair.

'They don't suit me at all. I always feel when I see them that I shall need to count the spoons more frequently.'

She was sitting in her usual chair, but seemed more sunken in it, more dependent upon it for support. She had never had much colour, but now she looked ashen. Events of recent days seemed to be catching up on her. The aquiline nose was more bony, the skin tighter on her face and forehead, and her hands and delicate fingers more fragile and transparent. Only the eyes had not changed; dark, shining, intelligent, missing nothing.

'Before we discuss anything else, can you tell me how Waldo and his wife are faring? When are they coming home?'

'I don't know, Miss Keelagher. I've kept in touch with the French police. I was informed to-day that matters are likely to become more serious for them. They are, at present, under house arrest but the magistrate in charge of the case is growing impatient. He is also apprehensive about allowing them to remain in a hotel. You will understand. Should they leave the hotel and get away, he will be in a difficult position. He thinks they ought now to be arrested and put in gaol. Suspicion naturally rests on Waldo. And unless we can file information which will allay or refute this suspicion, the French police will begin to make a case against your nephew. I'm sorry about that. The French police have been very patient and considerate, but it can't go on indefinitely.'

'I know. I read French detective stories...'

She gripped the arms of her chair tightly.

'And now, why are you calling on me? To busy men like you, this is not, I'm sure, a social call.'

There was a hush. Not a sound in the big house, as though, it, too, were waiting for what was coming next.

'Miss Keelagher, we know that you were in the vicinity of the crime, not far from Cannes, at the time it was committed. Will you kindly tell us why you were there and what you were doing?'

She showed no fear or surprise. Her eyes even grew a bit brighter and she gave Littlejohn a look of mild admiration.

'You have really found that out. I wish you would tell me how you did it.'

'The taxi drivers here and in France have identified you. You were absent from home at the time. You might satisfy my curiosity on one point before I go any further. How did you walk all the way from Mandelieu to Les Adrets? It is more than five miles there and five back. You must be gifted with remarkable grit and energy.'

It might have been a friendly chat. She seemed in no way antagonistic or on her guard. In fact, she might have been helping the police in the case.

'Of course I didn't walk. Dressed like the widow at a funeral, I inspired pity. As soon as I had the taxi out of sight, I thumbed a lift almost to Les Adrets. I speak excellent French, although I say so myself. I was educated at Le Puy, where an aunt of mine lived. She'd married a Frenchman. I'd no difficulty in getting a lift both ways. I went out on a petrol tanker and back in a Mercedes. They both thought I lived in a house off the main road near where they dropped me and picked me up. I told them I did.'

'This is going to be rather difficult, Miss Lucy. I have more questions to ask you, but you need not answer them. I must, however, warn you that any answers you give or anything you say may be used in evidence later... You understand?'

'Of course. This is what is known as "the caution", isn't it? I would have been disappointed in you if you had forgotten it.'

Cromwell was in torment. Miss Lucy was an adopted distant relative and he had grown fond of her. Yet, he had insisted on being with Littlejohn and now he was beginning to rue it.

'You did kill your brother, didn't you?'

'Yes, I did.'

No scenes, no excitement. She just admitted it in a matter-of-fact way, as though she'd already made up her mind what to do and could now face it without fear or emotion.

'Why?'

'This is going to be the ordeal now. Not the facts, but putting them in proper order and talking a lot. I'll try to be brief. He was always a bad boy when we were young. He was wanton and cruel. There was a streak of cruelty in our family. Cats, for example, affect *me* badly; I resent their composure and presumption. In the case of George, *everybody* seemed to affect him that way. He seemed to wish to defeat everybody, to be the cock, the dictator; to dominate their lives. As he grew older that became a kind of madness with him. He improved somewhat after he left school. My father, to whom he had been a great trouble and whom he hated because my father ceaselessly tried to discipline him, sometimes roughly, was delighted at the change. He soon regretted it, however. George, who entered the family firm, did so well in business, that my father retired before his time and made over his share to George. It was very foolish of him. He should have read *King Lear*. George quickly divested him of all he had and he had a stroke and was dependent on me. The story of Lear all over again.'

She told it as though she were paraphrasing something she'd read in a book.

'I never forgave him. I never spoke to George after that. We communicated by a stupid system of passing notes. George, I think, spied on me a lot. I'm sure he was responsible for the microphone system between my room and that of Richley, who, I presume, reported matters to him. It was clever of you to find it, Superintendent. As you know, it gave me a great shock when I learned it was there. I'd read about such things in my books, but never suspected they were in use in my house. The contraption is still there if you wish to examine it.'

'We know all about it, Miss Keelagher. There's one from Mr. George's room as well. Richley was the instigator of the eavesdropping.'

'I'm not surprised. They were a wicked pair. But I mustn't dwell on it. You wish to know why I killed George. Knowing him, I had to be a step ahead of George in everything. Otherwise, my own comfort, my old age, my very existence would have been in his hands. I couldn't allow that. I got the key of George's desk, as I told you. There is also that small safe in the corner of his room. That was my father's, too. George got all the keys for that, but not before I'd had a duplicate made of the one on father's key-ring. Now, I will briefly tell you how events led up to George's death. You will realise, won't you, that I would never have gone into all this, had you not told me that suspicion was likely to fall on Waldo? I had always been determined to make such a statement if anyone else fell under suspicion. I am trusting you and know that you've told me the truth about Waldo's position.'

'That is right. I give you my word on that.'

'George had determined that I should never marry. Not only did he want some insurance for his comfort in old age, but it was one of those things he delighted to do. To take another person's life and happiness and dominate them, ruin them. It does not make me angry to think of it now. He is dead and past being hated or punished. I think, if I may, I'll have some more tea. You are sure you would not care to join me. I won't embarrass you. I understand. You are on duty. Yes?'

They rang for tea for her. The German maid was surprised, but brought it. After Miss Lucy had settled down again, she resumed, precisely where she'd left off.

'George had a quiver full of baseness. He married his second cousin Elizabeth. I don't suppose any other girl would have him. He'd been engaged twice before, but both engagements were broken. They were lucky. One married and went abroad. The other went a bit queer after her affair with George and never married. I don't know why Elizabeth took George. I suppose it was for his money and she thought, as all young wives do, that she could change his very nature. She soon left him. Ran off with his partner, whom George later tried so hard to ruin, and, in the attempt, almost landed *himself* in gaol. Elizabeth now lives in Canada. You will probably know that George intended going to Canada to end his days ... *Did* you know? How wonderful! I wish I were a spectator to all this instead of a party. I would have better enjoyed studying your methods.'

'By the way, Miss Keelagher. Mr. Heller is in Charing Cross Hospital. He tried to commit suicide in, I imagine, an attempt to draw the trail in his direction instead of yours. When his attempt to take his own life failed, he made a full confession stating he murdered George Keelagher to break the blackmailing grip George had got on him ...'

Miss Lucy really looked pleased this time. She shed no tears nor made any scenes.

'I am very glad he did. It shows that he was a man, at least, instead of George's terrified rabbit. You didn't believe him?'

'His story was very credible. In fact, we might have believed it. But an alibi was forced upon him; an alibi he didn't want. I'm sorry, but his confession led us to you. There was no purpose in it if it wasn't to shield you. Heller had nobody else he greatly cared for but you and, I think, he was trying to make amends. He told us all about George's wicked interference between you and in his own life.'

'I don't blame Herbert for giving me away. I wouldn't have let him take the blame. But this is recompense for everything. Herbert Heller was prepared to hang or go to gaol for life for my sake. That's all right. It's as it should be.

George's death has freed him, at least, of his nightmare. He's a man again.'

'Was it George's interference between you and Heller and his treatment of Heller which made you finally decide to dispose of him?'

'That's a good word, Superintendent, and very tactful. Dispose of him. No. George finally decided to retire and to ruin Herbert Heller in the process. He wished to make sure that Herbert and I didn't make it up and that Herbert never became head of the firm of Keelagher and Heller. You know the financial mess in which George proposed to leave Herbert? Yes? That wasn't all. He'd gone off with twenty thousand pounds of Heller's money. I know that because, in his safe, George had all the calculations arising from his departure from the firm and what he proposed to do about it. He had an orderly mind and used to make lists of all he had to do. Even when he was at school he had that habit. He couldn't trust himself to remember all the villainies that crossed his mind. He had a list and ticked them off as he did them. I found such a list. I must tell you that Herbert has spoken with me twice recently. At first, I refused to see him. What was the use? But when I found that George had him in thrall, I agreed to talk with him. Herbert told me of the forged trust certificate he'd once issued to himself and how he'd overdrawn at the bank with the false trust shares as security and how George had found out and used the information to break-up our marriage plans and keep a hold over Herbert. On the list of his proposed ill-doings George had written "Send letter to Bank re forged certificate and tell solicitor to institute proceedings." You see, he was, after all he'd done to Herbert, going to see him in gaol in the end. And to make sure Herbert hadn't the money available to retrieve the forged share certificate before it was too late,

George blackmailed him to the tune of £20,000 which he took away with him. He didn't need that money. In his safe, I've seen evidence that he has deposits of over £50,000 in a Swiss Bank at Geneva. But all this talk may be a waste of time, Superintendent. I am only stating my motives. You have already proved my guilt.'

'Please go on, Miss Keelagher. It will help us to understand the case better. Did you recover the £20,000?'

'No. George was leaving the caravan with a small suitcase when I came upon him. After...afterwards, I took the suitcase away with me. It contained nothing but necessities for travelling. There was not a false bottom. I tore away the lining before I threw it away on a dump near Nice airport. I've no idea where the money is. Probably George had disposed of it through some doubtful channel and hoped to recover it somewhere on his travels. It may never turn-up now. That has made it necessary for me to provide the money from other sources. I have sold the jewellery in which I had invested much of my surplus funds, in secret to avoid George's spying, and paid the proceeds over to Herbert's bank to enable him to get back the spurious security. The letter to the bank notifying them of the fake security was in George's pocket. I took it and destroyed it. He was obviously going to post it after Herbert had settled-in as senior partner. George was determined to degrade him as much as he could. As if he hadn't done enough to him. When first I met Herbert, he was a well-built, good-humoured man. Look at him now. A nervous wreck and a complete misanthrope.'

'We know that you left here, took a taxi to the airport and travelled by the night 'plane to Nice. What happened then?'

'Waldo had sent me a postcard saying they were staying near Les Adrets for a few days. I looked it up on the map and I realised that I must act right away. I made my way to Les Adrets in the hope that some time before long Waldo and his wife would leave George to study his awful praying mantis on his own and give me a chance to talk with him. He had left England without saying goodbye. When I got up in the morning, he had packed his bags and gone. The previous evening Herbert Heller, whom I met in the park, away from Richley's eavesdropping, had told me about the £20,000 George had extorted from him and how it would ruin him. I determined next day to tackle George, once for all, break our long silence and, at least, see that Herbert was kept out of danger. Instead, George had gone and, it seemed, I would never see him again, for I had discovered his plans to go and live in Canada. The necessary papers had been in his safe for a few days and I went through them when he was out. I therefore had to follow George.'

'You came upon him at Les Adrets, ready packed for off?'

'Yes. He said he was in no mood for a tearful parting from Waldo. He was going to Nice airport in Waldo's car, if you please, leaving it in the park there, and getting the 'plane to New York where Father Martin would meet him. He taunted me for coming after him and trying to persuade him to release Herbert from his bondage. He said he had a letter denouncing Herbert to the bank, ready in his pocket for posting when he reached America. The letter would arrive just when Herbert thought he was rid of George for ever, and ruin him. George was still furious about Herbert's forging the certificate. He said it was an attempt to filch our family funds...As if George ever cared about the family! I asked him about the £20,000. He said I could have it if I could find it. He then pushed me aside and was making for the car. All this time there was nobody in sight and the occupants of the caravan seemed to be fast asleep. It was very dramatic.'

'I'm sure it was. How did you come to shoot him?'

'I didn't intend to do that...'

'Excuse me. Are you sure you didn't try to poison George with arsenic before he left home?'

She gave him a reproachful look.

'Certainly not. I thought I had satisfied Cousin Robert on that score. George had been trying to improve his health by taking arsenic in small doses. I showed Robert the book in which account is given of it. George had made notes in his medical diary about it. He kept a loose-leaf book in which he recorded his medical matters. He destroyed or otherwise disposed of all his papers; everything before he left. Perhaps he sent many of them to Canada. I don't know...'

'There was a small silver box containing arsenic in his pocket when he was found. That was yours, wasn't it?'

'If it was the one I think of, he must have taken it from my room. The pilferer! It stood on my dressing table. I'd missed it, but thought I'd misplaced it somewhere.'

'About the shooting. Did you take a revolver with you?'

She rose, opened a drawer, took out a revolver and gave it to Littlejohn.

'That is the one. I saw no point in disposing of it. It was my father's.'

It was a small, very old type of gun. It even fired pin-fire cartridges.

Littlejohn put it in his pocket.

'You were telling us what happened, Miss Keelagher.'

'When he pushed me aside, I took out father's revolver. I didn't even know it was loaded. It must have lain there for twenty years like that. I'd never fired one in my life, although I'd seen father use it. We once had some rats in the coalshed and he took it to dispose of them ...'

She was even light-hearted enough to laugh at that!

'... I remember his entering the coalshed and closing the door. Then there was a terrible fusillade of shots. It roused and alarmed the whole neighbourhood and the police called later. He did not kill the rats, which remained and multiplied until we had to call in the rat-catcher ...'

'You brandished the gun at George?'

'I had an idea of the technique from my reading. I pointed it at him and demanded the money and the letter. George seemed very amused and said something about my being as melodramatic as ever and snatched at the revolver. I must have been flurried, for I pulled at the trigger. George just fell where he stood, and lay there. The funny thing is that nobody heard it. The family in the caravan continued their sleep and everything was just as silent as before. There was a puff of smoke which vanished on the breeze. I took the letter, destroyed it there and then and put the bits in my bag, and went away with George's suitcase. As soon as I'd walked out of sight of the caravan, I stood on the main road for only a minute before a large car drew up and a Frenchman, driven by a chauffeur, offered me a lift. He dropped me just out of sight of the waiting taxi and then I came home. That seems to be all.'

'You think George was going to Canada to hunt down and pester his former wife?'

'I'm sure of it. He also proposed to spend a lot of time with Father Martin, a relative of ours who stayed over here last year. He, I think, must have given George the idea of going to Canada. Father Martin was a mild, kindly man, who seemed to get in George's black books for reproaching him about his way of life when he was with us here. George had made indignant notes in his diary about the things Martin had said to him. I found the diary among some erotic books which George kept locked in the safe...'

Littlejohn could imagine the grim game which had gone on between George and the sister who had grown to hate him. Following each other around; spying on one another; silent about it all; like a couple of merciless players each trying to checkmate the other.

'George was going to live with Martin, it seems.'

'Yes. And, I honestly believe, going to try to corrupt him, to undermine his faith. He was going to live in Martin's monastery for no good purpose. He was going as the devil's advocate, believe me.'

Nothing that George did or ever had done was of any good to Miss Lucy. Littlejohn realised that her mind had suffered in the game of perpetual hatred. Nobody would ever know how much was true and how much imagined.

'Is there anything more?'

'His will? How did he leave everything?'

'He had settled the heads of his will according to the notes, I found. Whether or not he signed it later, I couldn't find out. James, nothing; Waldo a share in the partnership, which George had already sold. The rest to charity. James and Waldo, however, will benefit under the family trust. George couldn't touch that. My father must, in creating it, have feared what George would try to do. George seemed to have left no assets of his own in England. The will was just an insult to the family and I suppose he proposed to dispose of his fortune in some way outside the will before his death. I don't know how. Certainly not charitably!'

'I think that is all. Cromwell has been making some notes and we will have a statement typed later and ask you to sign it...'

Poor Cromwell! He looked shattered and fumbled distractedly with his large black notebook.

'Don't worry, Cousin Robert. Superintendent Littlejohn will see that you don't suffer for my misdeeds, won't you, Mr. Littlejohn?'

'Of course I will. He is not involved in what you've done. He has done his duty splendidly.'

Cromwell had nothing to say.

'What is to happen now?'

'I'm sorry, Miss Lucy, but you'll have to accompany us. Will you ask Margaret to put some things together...?'

'Am I going to prison? Are you arresting me...?'

Miss Lucy Keelagher died the day after her arrest. Suffering from a chronic heart condition and sustained by tablets supplied by her doctor, she had, in apparent anticipation of what was ahead of her, abstained from taking her medicine. The emotion and shock had accelerated her end and she died in her sleep in her cell.

Months later, Waldo's missing car, sadly dismembered, suddenly appeared on a dump near Clermont-Ferrand. Nobody ever knew who put it there.

Herbert Heller, doubtless finding his bank account miraculously in credit again from an anonymous but well-guessed source, probably withdrew and hastily destroyed the nightmare share certificate, for nothing ever was made public about it.

In tracing George Keelagher's assets, the lawyers found the Swiss deposit, which had recently been augmented by £20,000. How George got it to Switzerland was always a puzzle. But there exist ways of doing such things to those in the know...

George left his fortune to what he called The Dogs' Home. Mr. Craddock had shared his little joke. Actually, it was a home for down-and-out old men, which Father Martin was planning to build in Montreal and he got his money in due course.

Another unsolved mystery was what George had proposed to do if he'd survived and reached Canada. Father Martin always believed he would have ended his days in the monastery guest-house, a wiser man, in search of peace and quiet. He was sure his earnest talks with George Keelagher had fallen on fruitful ground. He may have been right... Or, again, Miss Lucy might.

Two months after the sensation of the Keelagher affair had died down and Waldo was back in circulation again, another case appeared in odd corners of the newspapers. Eli Richley was arrested for bigamy. His real wife had been living in happy sin with another man for years, but, as she said in evidence, "I wouldn't have broke the law by marryin' again." The emotional appeal of Mrs. Benson in court, where she described Richley as a thorough gentleman, got him a sentence of a mere one day's imprisonment, and he left a free man with Mrs. Benson, to live in sin himself until it could be better arranged.

Littlejohn was in France again at the time and read all about it stretched in a long chair in the sunshine of Vence. He was called to the telephone, as before.

'This is Waldo Keelagher...'

Not again!

'Where are you?'

'In Cannes. We're spending an autumn holiday with the lawyer who helped us in August. Naturally, we sold the caravan! Can you and Mrs Littlejohn come over one evening for dinner? There's an urgent matter I want to discuss with you...'

Not another murder, surely? Perhaps James, this time?

'We're expecting a baby in Spring and we both want to know if you'll be godfather. We'll tell you all the details when we meet.'

Never a dull moment for Littlejohn!

Death of a Shadow

George Bellairs

Chapter One
The Unseen Watcher

'Will The owner of car with registration number GE 03567 parked in the English rose garden of the hotel, please remove it to the official car park?'

A quiet, determined, feminine voice came over the hidden loudspeakers in French and then repeated it in precise German and hesitant English.

Littlejohn heard it through a fug of cigar smoke and brandy. Like hearing the telephone in the middle of the night and trying to make out whether or not it's the alarm clock.

A pause. Everyone in the room looked around to discover if the culprit was there. Nobody reacted to the message and the hum of conversation and the rattle of coffee cups was resumed.

But the loudspeaker wasn't giving up so easily.

'Will the owner of car with registration number GE 03567...?'

French, German, English, to accommodate the cosmopolitan crowd of guests at the banquet.

Littlejohn took it all in again, but it didn't register. He was in that state of semi-trance which occurs after a mixture of good food, good wine, pleasant conversation and the babble of voices all around. He was also doing his best to answer questions about Elizabeth I's secret service, asked by the wife of the police chief of Madrid, whilst her husband tried to justify bullfighting to Mrs. Littlejohn. It was Mrs. Littlejohn who disturbed the conversation.

'Isn't that the number of *our* hired car?'

It was. Littlejohn confirmed it by a glance at the old envelope on which he'd recorded it. But he still hesitated. The whole business seemed ridiculous. What was the car doing in the sacred rose garden, of all places? He *had* put it in the official car-park under the palms and facing the lake, a small red *Sublime*, looking like a proletarian intruder wedged between a Rolls and a Cadillac.

'Will the owner of car...?'

It was like a third-degree. The loudspeaker was evidently determined to make somebody confess. Littlejohn excused himself to his friends, and rose. All eyes were upon him with complete sympathy, humour, good will, and a certain amount of admiration for his audacity. It was a dinner given to members of the police conference by the Geneva police and it added spice to the event that the English representative should commit a parking offence in the very middle of it. Littlejohn made his way through the crowded room and into the vast main hall of the *Hôtel du Roi*. It was packed with a milling throng. It was late May and although the holiday season had not yet opened, Geneva was overflowing with visitors. Four international conferences were in progress, Disarmament, International Cotton Manufacturers, Moral Improvement and Police. There were also a number of minor jamborees ranging from boy scouts to squabbling potentates from the Middle and Far East and Africa. People of all colours jostled for attention and space. Politicians, financiers, scientists, philosophers and cranks made speeches and attended banquets and parties. There were present at the police dinner fifteen Ministers of State from all over the world, including Sir Ensor Cobb, the British Minister of Security.

Outside, the night was clear and cool. The lights of Geneva and the resorts strewn round the edge of the lake competed with the stars. On the opposite side, at the head of the lake, the celebrated fountain cast up a floodlit jet of water which seemed to vanish in the outer darkness. An illuminated lake steamer waddled its way from Evian loaded with Moral Improvement delegates who had been celebrating there. The smell of the lake met Littlejohn as the revolving doors thrashed him out into the open. It was an all-pervading, nostalgic aroma, dear to all Genevese and other lovers of the city. To Littlejohn, it was a reminder of the damp stone floors of old English country houses.

The little car was right in the middle of the rose garden parked beside a fountain, with four dolphins spouting water at a naked nymph, and guarded by an indignant porter in uniform and gold braid. It looked at the same time, very small, lonely and impudent, the axis around which were incessantly revolving the splendid cars of the wealthy patrons of the hotel. It had been driven into the darkest part of the unlit garden, shaded by trees and flowering shrubs, as though the driver had wished to conceal the intrusion. The loudspeaker system was still in full blast. 'Will the owner of car with registration number GE 03567...?'

The porter didn't know Littlejohn but sensed that he was of the police. He was Swiss and trained to tolerate the antics of the eccentric. When he saw the joker was an Englishman his curiosity left him.

'I would have moved it, sir, but it is locked.'

That was all. No reproach, no demand for explanations. There would obviously be some financial recompense for his trouble and solicitude and the man was content to leave it at that.

But how had the thing got there? Locked, and the key in Littlejohn's pocket. Littlejohn unlocked the door with his key.

The first impression he got as he put his head in the car was a faint waft of perfume. It was certainly not that used by his wife. This was more pungent and exotic. Something probably with a name like *Passion, Toujours à toi,* or *Amour Furtif!* He switched on the interior light of the car.

Then he saw the bundle in the back. A triangular erection under the car rug. He removed the rug, and there it was. The body of a man, dumped on the back seat in a sitting posture knees up, arms sagging, quite dead. The eyes were wide open and staring, as though death had come upon him suddenly and shockingly.

Littlejohn took a closer look and whistled through his teeth. The dead man was Alec Cling, the detective assigned, for some unknown reason, to protect Sir Ensor Cobb. Sprawling there, drawn up on himself, one hand still extended, as though making an appeal or emphasising a point, Cling still seemed alive. He was a man who had spent the bulk of his official life since the war in following V.I.Ps. all over the earth. He had earned his place not through social graces, but on account of his physical strength, assiduousness and cunning. His technique as an official bodyguard and unseen watcher had been superb. Now, someone more adept than he must have turned up and ended it.

Cling, with the open staring eyes in the back of the small car was not a big man; medium built and slim, in fact. Brown-skinned, hawk-faced, slightly bald, with a large fleshy mouth, and around fifty. He was very neatly dressed, as became his status, and invariably wore a smart slouch hat. The murderer had carefully placed the latter beside him on the seat.

Littlejohn took it all in very quickly. Cling had been killed by a single purposive blow from a blunt instrument on the back of his head before he even knew what had hit him. That was obvious. The blood had coagulated round the wound and there was none in the car. He had probably been killed elsewhere and dumped.

Littlejohn thought of the plethora of policemen he had left inside the hotel. Many of them very young and full of new ideas, scientific routine, paper work. They thought the old hands at the game, Littlejohn and his contemporaries, were out of date and slow. At a time when some of the advanced moderns were even talking about computers in the detection of crime, the methods of the old brigade were regarded as formless and catch-as-catch-can.

His friend Dorange from Nice was one of the party indoors and he vaguely wished he could have sent in for him, the best collaborator he had ever had and another who was now regarded as a bit *passé*. Instead, Littlejohn behaved like an ordinary citizen and sent the porter to bring a policeman who was patrolling the waterfront. A tall, fair young man, impeccably turned out in the Geneva fashion. He looked inside the car and withdrew, casting upon Littlejohn a reproachful look as though the Superintendent himself had committed the crime and thus disturbed the civilised reputation of the city. Littlejohn made haste to introduce himself. The young man drew himself up and saluted efficiently.

'Will you, monsieur...?'

'I'll wait here until you report the matter.'

The officer looked hastily in the direction of the hotel, as though wondering whether or not to go there, and erupt into the banquet and announce his alarming news. Then he changed his mind and pointed to a telephone box along the quai.

'I will telephone headquarters...'

'That would be better.'

One could imagine the commotion caused by casting a murder in the midst of the feasting policemen!

Littlejohn stood in the open air waiting for the next move. The lake was silent and still, like the blackcloth of a theatre, with the lights of buildings and the lamps of the promenade reflected in it. Somewhere, in the distance, an orchestra was producing nostalgic music on a battery of violins. On a seat in one corner of the forecourt two lovers obliviously locked in each other's arms.

Then the police arrived. A tall, dark inspector in uniform, with close-clipped hair, two detectives, and an elderly man, evidently a doctor, with a shrivelled skin and a cough which he got off his chest repeatedly without removing his cigarette.

Littlejohn introduced himself to the inspector and gave him the key of the car. They spoke in French.

'I'll give you a statement when you're ready. The dead man in the car is called Cling and is the personal detective of Sir Ensor Cobb, who is, just now, present at the police banquet in the hotel.'

The young inspector was deferential.

'If you care to wait in the hotel, sir, I'll meet you in the hall in a few minutes.'

'That will give me a chance to let Sir Ensor know what has happened and explain my absence to my wife.'

Indoors, the news hadn't yet leaked out and the banquet was still going on. Sir Ensor was on his feet, reading a speech in halting French. The light from the great chandeliers above him made his bald head glow incandescently.

'... In these days of scientific progress, of high ideals, of enhanced public welfare, the fate of world civilisation is still in the hands of the police ...'

And he leaned forward and made a gesture like a pat on the back of every policeman present.

In the face of such eloquence and profound sentiments the tragic death of Alec Cling seemed pathetic and small. There, was, however, nothing to be done but to prick the bubble and bring Sir Ensor down to earth. Littlejohn scribbled a note on a leaf of his diary, tore it out, and sent it to the chairman, Dr. Sorgius, an eminent Swiss criminal lawyer, by a *chasseur*.

Dr. Sorgius looked surprised at the interruption and, still under the spell of Cobb's eloquence, absent-mindedly fished in his pocket and handed the astonished flunkey a two-franc piece for his services. He awoke, however, when he read the note.

Sir Ensor Cobb's detective, Cling, has just been found murdered outside this hotel.

Dr. Sorgius hesitated. Hoaxes of this kind were becoming a little too frequent and he called back the footman and asked him whence he'd got the message. The man pointed to Littlejohn, now standing at the door awaiting results. Littlejohn nodded in confirmation.

The chairman, known as a man of direct action, at once seized Sir Ensor's coat-tails and dragged him down from his flights of fancy. He then handed Cobb the note.

The effect was remarkable. Sir Ensor was a florid man with a pear-shaped body, long legs and a large bald head fringed by silver hair. He tottered at the news, the blood drained from his features, leaving them pale and lined with purple veins. He seemed suddenly to grow old and afraid. Dr. Sorgius snapped his fingers at the head waiter, who, reading his thoughts, advanced upon Sir Ensor and gave him brandy, which didn't seem to improve his condition at all, for he sank lower in his chair, as though settling himself for a nap.

The guests in the body of the banqueting hall sat, at first, like an audience awaiting the resumption of a film show after a power-cut. They didn't know what had happened. Many of them had seen Littlejohn scribble and hand the note to Dr. Sorgius and the effect it had produced. Some wondered if the British government had fallen; others if some kind of disgrace had fallen upon Sir Ensor.

Dr. Sorgius rose to dispel their curiosity.

'I fear we must now end the proceedings. I regret to inform you that Sir Ensor Cobb has suffered a bereavement...'

There was a rumble of condolence among the guests.

That was too much for Cobb. He'd never liked Cling, who had been thrust upon him after he had received anonymous telephone calls and letters threatening him with bombs and bullets. He rose unsteadily to his feet, for he'd consumed a goblet full of brandy. He wasn't having anyone thinking Cling was a close relative of his. He held up his hand for silence. You could have heard a pin drop, except that in the kitchens somebody was singing *Capri* in robust *bel canto*.

'I regret that I am unable to finish my speech. My personal detective has been found dead outside this hotel and it would appear to be murder...'

Almost a dozen reporters rushed out to the nearest telephones, on their ways concocting stories, supplementing from imagination what they hadn't learned in fact. Some of them even approached Cobb for a statement and a television squad with full apparatus glided down upon him for a close-up news conference. Dr. Sorgius chased them all away.

Having delivered his bombshell, the Minister of Security sagged again, seemed to lose all interest in what was going on and was assisted unsteadily from the room.

It was then that the newspaper correspondents realised that Littlejohn was big news, but they were too late, for the Swiss police arrived and led him away.

Want another Perfect Mystery?

Get your next Classic Crime Story for FREE ...

Sign up to our Crime Classics newsletter where you can discover new Golden Age crime, receive exclusive content and never-before published short stories, all for FREE.

From the beloved greats of the golden age to the forgotten gems, best-kept-secrets, and brand new discoveries, we're devoted to classic crime.

If you sign up today, you'll get:

1. A Free Novel from our Classic Crime collection.
2. Exclusive insights into classic novels and their authors and the chance to get copies in advance of publication, and
3. The chance to win exclusive prizes in regular competitions.

Interested? It takes less than a minute to sign up. You can get your novel and your first newsletter by signing up on our website www.crimeclassics.co.uk

Printed in Great Britain
by Amazon